SHAPE-
SHIFTER

SHAPE-SHIFTER

STORIES BY

Pauline Melville

PANTHEON BOOKS   NEW YORK

The author wishes to thank
Rhonda Cobham Sander and Margaret Busby
for their helpful comments on these stories.

Copyright © 1990 by Pauline Melville

All rights reserved under International and Pan-American Copyright Conventions.
Published in the United States by Pantheon Books, a division of Random House, Inc.,
New York. Originally published in the United Kingdom by The Women's Press
Limited, London in 1990.

Library of Congress Cataloging-in-Publication Data

Melville, Pauline.
Shape-shifter : stories / Pauline Melville.
  p.   cm.
I. Title.
PR6063.E445S48   1991
823'.914—dc20   91-52621
ISBN 0-679-40438-4

Manufactured in the United States of America

First American Edition

TO MY PARENTS

CONTENTS

The shape-shifter can conjure up as many different
figures and manifestations as the sea has waves.

Unknown poet

It is a firm article of faith that the shaman or medicine-man
of the Indians of Guiana, to whom nothing is impossible,
can effect transformation of himself or others.

Walter Roth, Enquiry into the Animism and
Folklore of the Guiana Indians

I DO NOT TAKE MESSAGES FROM DEAD PEOPLE

Shakespeare McNab waited in the outer office of the Ministry of Home Affairs. His appointment with the Vice-President of the Republic had been for eleven o'clock. It was now half past. He had no idea why he had been summoned. The secretary had been unable or unwilling to enlighten him. Shakespeare smiled ingratiatingly whenever she looked up from her typewriter and she ignored him. He took some papers from the briefcase on his knee and pretended to study them. The rambling, wooden building in which he waited was one of the old, colonial houses built by the plantocracy and now converted into government offices and ministries. Outside, the gracious width of the street was divided along its length by a stagnant canal. At intervals of fifty yards or so, giant royal palms sported mangy and yellowing foliage. Shakespeare decided that secretaries to public officials ought to be given a course in charm. He would not reprimand her for being ungracious. He would simply shame her with the exquisiteness of his own manners. She paused from her typing and looked up. Shakespeare gave his most delightful smile. She resumed typing with some ferocity. He fanned himself with his papers. It was hot and he was thirsty.

'The Comrade Vice-President will see you shortly.' The secretary did not raise her eyes as she spoke. Shakespeare experienced a flicker of anxiety. Could it be that someone at the broadcasting station where he worked had reported him for not using the term 'Comrade' frequently enough when addressing his colleagues? He prepared his defence. He was a broadcaster. It befitted him to be accurate in his use of words. His dictionary had informed him that the word 'comrade' was supposed to refer to 'a close companion' or 'an intimate associate', not any old Tom, Dick or Harry as was the custom nowadays. Besides, the Vice-President would hardly be summoning him for a personal interview on such a trivial matter. No, it was bound to be something of more weight. Perhaps the Vice-President was looking for someone to write his official biography. That would be a more appropriate reason for the summons. Shakespeare worried over how he would deal with the widespread and malicious rumour that the Vice-President had been responsible for the death of his own wife, by poison, at a state banquet after she had threatened to reveal certain delicate facts about his financial acquisitions during the current term of government. One moment, apparently, she had been toasting the Republic and the next she was slumped, face down, in a silver dish of curried shrimps. Shakespeare frowned. We allow too much scandal and gossip to interfere with our politics, he thought. It is because we are a relatively young nation. We will mature in time. Although, he recollected, she had been cremated, which was unusual. And with surprising haste.

Shakespeare shifted along the bench to the part that was shaded from the window. If he were truly to be offered the post of Comrade Biographer to the Comrade Vice-President, no doubt he would be required to give some details about his literary accomplishments:

'Of course, there are my two volumes of poetry. The muse does visit me occasionally, usually at night . . .' Shakepeare paused in his thoughts. The enormous hulk of the Vice-President did not seem to be the sort of shape whose owner would be interested in verse. He was puzzled. Why should the Vice-President be interested in what he, Shakespeare, was best known for – the collecting of folk-lore? Each morning, after the nine o'clock news, Shakespeare came on the air with a proverb or saying from one of the cultural traditions of the nation: African, Asian, Chinese, Amerindian, Portuguese or Dutch. On Thursdays, he had a ten-minute slot and told a longer folk story. Today was Friday. He had just finished a short proverb when Horace Tinling, his boss, put his head round the door of the small cubicle that passed for a studio and informed him that he was wanted immediately at the Ministry of Home Affairs. Shakespeare disliked Horace Tinling. In his opinion, a man who wore a bow tie with his camouflage jacket was a special sort of hypocrite. It occurred to him now that he was possibly going to be asked to replace Horace Tinling as Head of Home Programmes. Satisfaction bloomed inside him. He began to rehearse in his head the expansive, man-to-man chat he thought would take place as he was granted this new status. Hopefully, over a cool drink:

'How did I come to be called Shakespeare? Well, Comrade Vice-President, the story is that when I was born, my father came home from work, looked at me and said: 'Well, he don' look so bright. 'E ain' pretty either. We better do something to help him make his way in the world. We goin' name 'im Shakespeare.' And, in fact, I did turn out to have some small literary talent.' Shakespeare liked to end this anecdote with a self-deprecating chuckle. He imagined the Vice-President chuckling with him as they sipped their drinks – drinks served by the secretary who would be forced to alter her aloof demeanour to one of friendly respect when she witnessed the intimate camaraderie between the two men. On the other hand, perhaps it would be wiser not to mention names. The Vice-President's name was Hogg. Shakespeare had attended the same school as Hogg, who was a few years his senior. His most distinct memory of the Comrade Vice-President was of him leading the school choir on Empire Day in a lusty rendition of 'Here's a Health unto His Majesty. Fal la la la la Fa la la la.' It would not be tactful to remind him of that either. But he must remember to congratulate him on his recent appointment to the prestigious post of Vice-President, the only other serious contender for the post having been found shot dead in Camp Street.

'The Comrade Vice-President will see you now.' The secretary was holding the door open.

Shakespeare stood in the centre of the room, a deferential smile firmly in place on his impish features. The smile was not returned by the Vice-President, a heavily-built black man whose overpowering sullenness held the gravitational density of an imploding star. He remained behind the desk and stared at Shakespeare. Behind his head, on the wall, a formal portrait of the President himself, with pursed mouth and coptic eyes, smirked down at Shakespeare. The Vice-President rose to his feet and came round from behind the desk. Despite his weight, his hips swivelled freely, like those of a spoilt schoolgirl. He came unhesitatingly forward and delivered a resounding slap to the left side of Shakespeare's face:

'Be more careful what stories you broadcast in future, Comrade McNab. That's all. Good morning.'

Green with fright, Shakespeare McNab left the office.

Shakespeare made his way past the secretary to the door, his features frozen in a paralysed, lop-sided rictus, exactly as the slap had left them. He hoped the secretary would mistake the immobile gawp on his face for some sort of farewell smile. Speech was beyond him. He stumbled down the wooden stairs into the street. It was mid-day and there were not many passers-by but Shakespeare had the distinct impression that each one of them knew what had just happened to him, as if someone was riding alongside him on a bicycle with a megaphone, announcing: 'THIS MAN HAS JUST BEEN SLAPPED ROUND THE FACE BY THE VICE-PRESIDENT OF THE REPUBLIC.' His trembling legs moved forward along the grass verge without seeming to make progress, like a mime-walker. 'What did I do? What did I do?' he repeated over and over. Usually, the heat and the spaciousness of the street conspired to reduce the most hurried pace to a stroll, but fear and the desire to put as much distance as possible between himself and the Vice-President propelled Shakespeare across one of the small canal bridges, towards the centre of town. His khaki shirt tail flapped behind him. 'What did I do? What did I do?' he asked himself, over and over again.

Instinctively, he headed for home. By the time he reached the ancient iron structure of the old Dutch slave market, a dreadful realisation had begun to dawn on him of a blunder that he might have made, a bloomer of such horrific enormity that the edges of his mind began to tingle. He attached himself to a group of people who had gathered under the pitiless sun, encouraged by the rumour of a bus, but agitation made him incapable of standing still for more than a minute or two and soon he continued, walking briskly away from the heart of the city. What had occurred to him was this:

Yesterday had been a Thursday, the day he regularly broadcast one of his longer folk stories. General laziness had prevented him from preparing the programme in advance. The studio clock was already pointing at ten to nine when he burst into the recording cabin, treading over the chaotic jumble of spools, reel-to-reel tapes and story-books. In this sort of emergency, he usually resorted to telling an Anancy story – Anancy, the regional folk-hero, the magic spider with the cleft palate and the speech defect, the tricksy creature of unprepossessing proportions who continually outwitted the great and savage beasts of the jungle. He grabbed a book of Anancy stories from the shelf and flicked through the pages to find one that he had not already read. Unfortunately for him, the one he plumped for was entitled 'Anancy and Hog'.

'Good morning, Guyana. And it is another beauuuuuuutiful day in our co-operative socialist republic, so I goin' tell you the story of Anancy and Hog.

'One day Anancy and 'im grandmamma go to a ground fi provision. Anancy left him guitar there. When 'im comin' home togedder wid him grandmamma, he said: "Grandmumma, you know I did leave my guitar at groun'." Him grandmamma say: "Me son, you is a very bad boy. Go for it but don' play it."

'When Anancy comin' home he play:

> "When you see a hugly man,
> When you see a hugly man
> When you see a hugly man
> Never mek him marry you sister."

Then him hear footstep. Him lift up one of 'im legs an' listen. Along come Hog. Hog say: "Brother, you a play de sweet, sweet tune." Anancy say: "No, Bro'er." Hog say: "Play, mek me hear." Anancy play Bap, Twee, Twee, Twee, all wrong note. Hog suck 'im teeth and say: "Tcho! You caan play." Hog pass by. As 'im walk pon de road 'im hear Anancy playing the tune. Hog come back: "Brother Anancy, I think you a play, you beggar. I goin' kill you.'' An' Hog carry home Anancy an' goin' do him up for him dinner because that night he plan one big feast wid plenty big-wig hog comin' fi supper. But inside de house, Anancy pop off de rope an' dress up in Hog wife clothes. An' 'im say to Hog wife: ''If you waan look pretty put on me lickle black suit an' shut up you mouth!'' An' then Hog come in an' kill 'im own wife. An' when Hog think 'im done up Anancy, 'im done up 'im own wife and serve her for supper. And that is what make Hog a nasty feeder up to this day.

'Well, that's all from me for today. This is Shakespeare McNab signing off until tomorrow.'

As Shakespeare remembered precisely what he had broadcast the day before and the implications for his good health, he came to a halt on the corner of Howard and Queen Street. Some warm slops, thrown by a woman from the verandah of her house, spattered him. He barely noticed. Vice-President Hogg, he thought, believes that I have announced to the nation the fact that he murdered his wife. Shakespeare licked dry lips and put on a final spurt for home.

Safely inside his one-storey house on stilts, Shakespeare moved quickly round lowering the jalousie slats on all the windows. It made the place intolerably hot but he felt less vulnerable that way. In near darkness, he made his way to the table and poured himself a stiff rum. Then he sat on the sofa alternately sipping the rum and biting his nails. Just as he was planning to make his next morning's broadcast a fulsome eulogy, extolling the virtues of Vice-President Hogg, the telephone rang. It was the smarmy voice of Horace Tinling giving him the sack:

'So sorry, Comrade . . . unforeseen circumstances . . . replacing you with a recipe programme . . . if you could clear out your belongings before nine o'clock on Monday night, when the Vice-President is due to give a ministerial broadcast.'

Shakespeare was too stunned to object. He went to the window and peered through one of the slats. His heart gave a flip. Parked on the other side of the street, opposite his house, was an unmarked car. Lolling up against it were three bulky Afro-Guyanese men, all wearing dark glasses. At the same time, he saw his friend, Denzil Bennet, bounding up the wooden steps to his front door:

'Why you sittin' in the dark?' enquired Denzil, helping himself to a glass of rum. Paranoia prevented Shakespeare telling Denzil what had happened:

'I got a headache . . . The light hurtin' me eyes.' Denzil flopped onto the sofa and ran his hands through his manic bush of frizzy, greying hair:

'You hear the latest story about Hogg?' he asked.

Shakespeare eyed him suspiciously:

'What story?' Had Denzil heard something, already? He came and sat on the sofa.

'Remember how we laugh at the Cuffy statue?' Denzil continued.

Shakespeare did indeed remember how they had laughed when the statue of the great slave leader had been unveiled. The statue was grasping a scroll in his hand, held at the hip, pointing upwards, but at such an angle that when the covering flag was pulled off, it appeared to a section of the crowd that Cuffy was holding himself with an enormous erection. Shakespeare recalled how he and Denzil had joined in the rippling titter that swept through the onlookers. Just now, however, he was unwilling to admit ever having laughed at anything organised by the government.

'Well,' Denzil went on, 'the story go so. One night Hogg's personal aide was contemplating the statue when the statue start to speak: "Get me a horse," says Cuffy. "You can't speak – you're a statue!" says the aide. "Get me a horse. In Berbice in 1763, I used to ride a horse." Well, the aide is so frighten, he run all the way to Hogg private residence. "Cuffy speakin'," he says. "The statue speakin'. Come look." Now, as you know, Hogg is an extremely superstitious man. He consult an obeah woman and all that foolishness. Apparently, she give him a special ring whose stone change colour when 'e life in danger. So now Hogg think 'e bein' given a special sign an' 'e pull on his pants an' come back with the aide to the statue. "Fool," says Cuffy to the aide. "I said I wanted a horse, not a jackass." '

Denzil let out a screech of laughter. Shakespeare remained silent. He felt sure that Denzil had been sent to trap him. Laughter in the present circumstances could be interpreted as a form of high treason.

'You don' think that funny?' Denzil stared at Shakespeare in disbelief. 'What's the matter with you, man? That headache eat out you brain or what?'

'I goin' to my bed,' announced Shakespeare, abruptly. 'My head is hurtin' me.' Denzil shrugged and swallowed the last of his rum.

'Tell me what you see in the street,' demanded Shakespeare as Denzil opened the door.

'There ain' nothin' in the street. Street empty. Go to bed, man. You sick.'

The door banged shut behind him, leaving Shakespeare in the gloom.

That night, Shakespeare tossed and turned under his single sheet like a cat in a sack. He suffered the most horrible nightmare. He dreamed he was standing on the sea wall. All around him he smelled the detritus of crab and shellfish left there by fishermen. As he gazed out over the waters of the Atlantic, a black shape began to emerge from the sea. It grew larger and larger, laughing in a sinister manner as it became gigantic. Then it sank back down in the sea and he saw the letters H O G G written in the sky. Shakespeare woke sweating from the dream. Too frightened to go back to sleep, he spent the rest of the night hugging up his knees with his arms, fretting over what to do.

The next morning, Shakespeare miserably cleared out his office, scooping his tapes and books into a large canvas bag. Horace Tinling watched him with an expression somewhere between mock sympathy and outright superciliousness. Replacing him in the recording studio was a smartly dressed, young black woman, leaning towards the microphone as she gave out a recipe for Yam Foo-Foo. On his way home, he called at his grandmother's house in Albuoystown. Nibbling at breadfruit cooked in coconut milk, he told her the whole sequence of events, including the dream of the night before. She was a woman of few words:

'Leave the country,' she said.

News travels fast in a country without the benefits of advanced communications technology. The whole of that Saturday and the following day, nobody came to call on Shakespeare. None of his friends appeared. The telephone remained mute. It was as if, overnight, he had become a leper. Taking advantage of the unaccustomed solitude, Shakespeare pored over his dilemma. He went over every detail of what had happened to him. He recalled Denzil's scorn of Hogg's superstitious cast of mind. He recalled Hogg's appointment at the radio station. Late on Sunday evening, the first faint inkling of an idea came to him, an idea for his deliverance so wild and fantastical that he put his hand over his mouth and shook his head. 'No, I couldn't,' he thought. 'Yes, I could. No, it's outrageous . . . Yes, I will.'

As the Monday morning vendors laid out their pyramids of scarlet wiri-wiri peppers and green water melons for the day's sale, Shakespeare was already knocking at the door of his grandmother's house.

'You wan' coffee-tea, cocoa-tea or tea-tea? I ain' got milk.' She shuffled round the tiny kitchen.

'Tea-tea,' said Shakespeare. It was his next request that she balked at. She jutted out her jaw and looked at him askance:

'Why you want to borrow me clothes?' she asked, suspiciously.

Shakespeare avoided an explanation. He cajoled and begged his grandmother until finally she gave in and let him depart with one longish skirt, an old blouse with puffed sleeves, a headwrap and a pair of high-heeled shoes her daughter had abandoned there the year before.

On his way home, Shakespeare bought an old coconut. Once inside the house, he allowed the jalousies to remain shut and moved around in semi-darkness. Every now and then he checked through a slat to see if the unmarked car with its ominous occupants had reappeared. No sign of them. He emptied the tapes and books from his bag onto the sofa and replaced them with the clothes his grandmother had lent him. Then he chopped the coconut in half and cut out the white flesh with a small knife. After that, he spent some time banging the two halves of the shells together until they produced a sound that satisfied him. Then he placed those too inside the bag. He fetched an axe and that also went in the bag. 'Now comes the difficult bit,' he said to himself, and went over to the telephone. Several times he lifted the receiver and replaced it on the hook. Each time he put it back, he would walk round the room rehearsing a slightly different version of what he planned to say. Finally, he picked up the phone and dialled the number of Vice-President Hogg's office. The secretary answered.

'Good morning.' The tone of Shakespeare's voice was fawning. 'This is Comrade Shakespeare McNab speakin'. I am so sorry to trouble you – I would not dream of troublin' you if it was not a matter of extreme urgency. I have had a warning dream concerning the Vice-President. My dead mother appeared to me in a dream last night warning me that he is in imminent danger and I felt it my duty to pass the message on.'

There was a moment's hesitation on the other end of the line, then came the snappy reply:

'I do not take messages from dead people.'

Shakepeare's brain raced. His entire plan would totter if the message did not get through:

'No. The message is from ME,' he said, hastily. And to ensure that the Vice-President did, indeed, receive the information, he added, 'I shall, of course, be writing to confirm what has happened, but I thought I should pass it on as quickly as possible, lest anything should occur before the letter reaches him. I should not like to be the one responsible for withholding that sort of information.' That should fix her, thought Shakespeare, who discovered to his surprise that he was on his knees in front of the telephone.

'All right.' The voice was reluctant. 'I shall inform the Comrade Vice-President if you think it is really necessary.'

'Thank you,' said Shakespeare. 'I think it is.' His scalp was tingling all over as he hung up.

More than once, during the rest of the afternoon, Shakespeare decided to abandon his plan altogether. It was too risky. Too much was at stake. It would be wiser to do what his grandmother suggested and flee the country. Nobody would offer him a decent job if he could not get his old one back, and if this scheme failed, he could say goodbye to the broadcasting world forever. All the same, perhaps it was worth one last attempt.

As dusk fell, a shortish man could be observed sizing up and examining the trees that bordered a narrow stretch of road some distance from the city. To his right, the road led to the entrance gates of Vice-President Hogg's private residence. The house itself remained out of sight at the end of a long drive. To his left, the road extended for a hundred yards or so until it met the main highway. Nothing but a tangle of trees and shrubs stood on either side of it. Overhead, a host of bats sewed up the great opal and silver clouds with their flitting, looping trajectories. Half way between the gates and the end of the road, Shakespeare spotted the tree that he wanted. It was a young, slender casuarina tree. He took the axe from the bag and began to chop at the base of the trunk. With the sound of each chop, his heart leapt with fear and he glanced up and down the road. No one came. When the trunk was half severed, Shakespeare looked at his watch and decided to wait. He hid out of sight, in the bushes. The tree stayed upright. At about the time he had estimated, a chauffeur-driven limousine turned off the main road and made its stately way up the rutted earth track towards the entrance to Hogg's estate. The driver stopped to unlock the gates and then the car disappeared up the drive. It was nearly dark.

'Quick. Quick. Is now or never,' whispered Shakespeare to himself, his face set in a wild grimace. With all his might, he pushed at the trunk of the casuarina tree until it fell in a graceful faint, blocking the road. Shakespeare dissolved back into the bushes, then remembered he had left his bag by the tree, ran to retrieve it and slipped on some wild tamarind pods. He cursed, but the pods gave him an idea. He picked one up and shook it. It rattled. He slipped it under his arm and melted once more into the trees. The sky had turned from silver to grey to black.

Vice-President Hogg gazed moodily from the open back window of his limousine as the driver came to a halt, the branches of the toppled casuarina tree waving in his headlights:

'I have to get some help to move this obstruction,' apologised the driver after inspecting the offending tree. Hogg grunted his assent and waited while the chauffeur sped off towards the main road.

It was then that Hogg began to hear things. First of all he heard the sound of soft, ploppy bangs on the roof of the car which he dismissed as something falling from the trees. Then, what appeared to be the piercing whistle of a bird assailed his ears, a whistle that ended in an unearthly rattle. Two minutes later, from his right, he heard a loud munching sound from the bushes. Almost immediately, from his left he heard a high-pitched voice calling:

'Hello, daalin'.'

Silence followed. Hogg's small eyes shifted from side to side. Nothing happened. Hogg permitted himself to relax a fraction when the silence was broken by the clip-clop of hooves along the dried earth road. Hogg thrust his head out of the car window. What he saw appalled him. Beyond the section of road, illuminated by the car headlights, he could just make out the figure of a woman. She wore some kind of headwrap and a whitish dress with puffed sleeves. She was approaching slowly with a lolloping, uneven gait. Worst of all, she was beckoning him with the crook of her first finger, beckoning him to follow her into the bushes. Hogg gave a little moan and fell on his knees in the back of the car. No sooner had he assumed this position than all hell seemed to break loose in the trees at the side of the car. He could hear shouts, the crashing of branches and the snapping of twigs, as if some enormous creature was threshing about. Then Hogg heard a familiar voice yelling:

'Go way! Leave him alone, I tell you.' More silence.

Fearfully, Hogg raised his face to the window where it confronted the equally tense face of Shakespeare McNab.

'Praise the Lord. You safe.' Shakespeare panted. 'Did you get my message? I came to warn you in case the message din reach.'

Hogg wiped a film of sweat from his face with a handkerchief. The breast of his khaki jacket rose and fell as he stared, mesmerised, at Shakespeare, his jaw slack.

'Might I get in the car? I think it would be safer for both of us.' Shakespeare tried to control his breathing rate. Hogg shifted to the far side of the back seat and Shakespeare slipped in beside him:

'Lord a mercy. All these years I bin tellin' stories about these things an' I never really believe them. Now I know it all true. Lucky I was here. I fought her off. You know who that was?'

Hogg's eyes swivelled towards Shakespeare. They seemed to contain some sort of warning, but Shakespeare could not stop:

'La Diablesse.'

'Who?' asked Hogg, confused.

'La Diablesse.' Shakespeare lowered his voice to a whisper. 'That must have been the warning my mother was trying to give you in the dream. Did you get the message I left?'

Hogg nodded.

'La Diablesse. You know. She got one straight foot and one cloven hoof. She lure people to their death in the forest.'

A rumbling laugh emerged from Hogg's nether regions. Shakespeare quailed. The plan was not working. Hogg didn't appreciate the seriousness of an encounter with La Diablesse. Shakepeare's own heroism would go for naught. He shot a worried glance at Hogg's enormous, shaking bulk.

'Jesus God,' said Hogg. 'I thought it was my wife.'

The strength oozed out of Shakespeare's limbs. Never had it occured to him that Hogg would mistake the apparition for the ghost of his wife. He attempted to put the matter right:

'If you will forgive me for contradicting you, Comrade Vice-President, I am sure that what I saw was La Diablesse. When I shouted and shake the branches, she jus' fade back into the trees.'

Hogg frowned. 'What brought you here?' He sounded suspicious.

'A feelin'. A powerful feelin',' said Shakespeare.

Shakespeare peered timorously at the corpulent figure beside him. Hogg appeared preoccupied. He was scowling as he fingered the ring on his right hand, twisting it this way and that. Suddenly, he pulled the ring off and flung it through the car window. Just then, the car headlights picked out the anxious face of the chauffeur. He was with another man and together they set about removing the tree from the path of the car. Shakespeare knew that if he was to seize the opportunity before it vanished he would have to make his move fast:

'Well, sir . . . Comrade sir, I can see that you are safe now. I must be gettin' home. Sadly, I have been made redundant from the broadcasting station and I have got to get up early and look for other work.'

Hogg turned slowly and scrutinised Shakespeare. Shakespeare wilted a little under the penetrating stare.

'I have an idea,' said Hogg, thoughtfully. 'I think I might be able to help you on this.'

Shakespeare batted his eyelids and started to thank him effusively, hoping for an immediate return to the broadcasting station, but Hogg continued: 'I am going to offer you a position as my personal adviser.'

In his grandmother's kitchen the next day, Shakespeare strutted from the window to the table, laughing and boasting as he related, in full detail, the success of his ruse:

'So, what you think, grandmumma. I clever? You grandson clever? I am now Personal Adviser to Comrade Vice-President Hogg,' he crowed.

She stirred some casreep into the pepper-pot.

'Leave the country,' she said.

'I am marooned, Molly!'

Donella Saunders stood on the verandah and gazed across the dried patch of garden towards the neighbouring house. That house, like her own, needed a coat of paint. The white wooden building sagged in places. Rust had crept over the zinc roof of the outhouse. The stake fence between the two properties zig-zagged all askew under the weight of untrimmed hibiscus that ran along its length.

The plump white woman with a necklace of mosquito bites around her neck sat in the wicker chair and said nothing.

'I cannot imagine why you came,' continued Donella. 'We are in a parlous situation here. Extremely parlous.'

A brown-skinned woman in her mid-fifties, she was tall, extraordinarily thin, with a high forehead and an air of ravaged elegance. Her wavy brown hair was scraped back from her face and pinned untidily with combs. She flicked ash from her cigarette nervously into the garden and stared morosely ahead of her at nothing in particular.

Molly Summers basked in the satisfaction of knowing precisely why she was there in the sun-struck capital of Guyana. It was in order to enrich the lives of the schoolchildren she taught in England. Only half-aware of the other woman's mood, she sipped a cold cup of coffee and inspected her new sandals. She tried to imagine the shoe shop in Finsbury Park where she had bought them, continuing business as usual while she sat thousands of miles away on the other side of the Atlantic.

From the first moment when, some years ago now, she had muttered 'Oh yes Lord' in the silence and tranquillity of the

Friends' Meeting House in Muswell Hill, she had recognised her mission: to work for, understand and promote the culture of the oppressed races in England; to ensure equality of treatment at least as far as Moseley Road Junior School was concerned – she had even proposed (unsuccessfully) that the name of the school be changed. By nature a self-effacing woman, she overcame her timidity to make frequent interventions at staff meetings. She attended all the anti-racist courses run by the local education authority and cast reproving looks at colleagues who made racially ambiguous statements. She studied the pre-emancipation history of the West Indies, experiencing quiet satisfaction at the role of the Quaker movement in the struggle against slavery. The Quaker faith suited her with its one god so pale and subdued and down to earth that he barely existed. High self-esteem was an abomination to Molly, who trod a lifelong tightrope between trying to do good and trying not to feel pleased with herself for having done so. But as far as the race question went she prided herself on having got it pretty much right. When the opportunity to visit the West Indies came in the form of a remark made casually by the only black teacher in the school – who never dreamed that it would be taken up and acted upon – that if Molly really wanted to visit the Caribbean she could probably stay with her brother, Molly leapt at it. It was her duty to go. She battened down her feelings of apprehension and consulted her colleague on appropriate clothing.

And here she was.

It was ten in the morning. The sun was manoeuvring itself into position for the mid-day strike and Molly felt a prickling sensation along her forearms as if tiny, crystalline needles were being inserted under the skin. She raised a chubby hand and patted the top of her head. If only someone had reminded her to bring some sort of hat. Her pleasant, unremarkable face was framed by a neat helmet of iron grey hair, cut pudding basin style with a fringe. When she smiled, her expectant expression combined with the childish haircut made her look like one of those fuzzy newspaper photos of a murdered ten-year-old girl. She was, in fact, fifty-nine years old.

Donella pulled her yellow kimono round a body that was all angles like a stick insect and addressed Molly:

'Excuse my *déshabillée*. You must forgive me. My mind too is disorganised this morning.' The accent was extravagently English upper-class, hardly a trace of Guyanese, the result of years spent in England, daughter of some high-ranking diplomat. She stood facing Molly, taking short nervy puffs at her cigarette.

'The iron and the radio have gone,' she announced. 'Someone climbed in through the window. I am totally unnerved. Completely and utterly unnerved. Do you think the maid left the top half of the door unlocked or did they come in through the window? On top of everything, this is the last straw. The radio I can do without, but not the iron. The iron cost three hundred dollars. We have nothing here. I am distraught.'

She wafted from the verandah into the living room to look for an ashtray. In a minute, she returned:

'Excuse me, dear. Here are some magazines for you to look at.' She tossed some ancient copies of *Harper's* magazine and a *Tatler* onto the table. 'I am afraid the telephone is constantly demanding my attention.'

Molly could hear her dialling a number on the telephone and then heard the wailing voice relating the story of the iron and the radio. She had been dumped at Donella's house by her reluctant host, Ralph Rawlings, while he went about some business downtown. As soon as he returned she would persuade him to drop her at a bookshop where she might find some educational material to take home. She had begun collecting small items like a magpie, postcards, Amerindian artefacts, the sort of thing that would be a stimulus in the classroom. Now she needed books. Story books and picture books.

She picked up a magazine idly and put it down again. A fat, old, black woman came onto the verandah of the house opposite and threw something from a pot into the garden. Heat pinioned Molly to her seat. She remembered the night she had arrived at Timehri Airport. Nothing had prepared her for the beauty of Georgetown. The streets were the widest she had ever seen. Tall slender Royal Palms tapered off into the sky, the foliage of each one silhouetted against the night clouds like a spider dancing on a stick. The taxi passed stylish old colonial buildings whose latticed partitions and verandahs gave the appearance of white wooden lace and then continued, carrying her across small bridges over intersecting canals. But the next morning she awoke to find the city smiling at her with rotting teeth. She was living in an open sewer. A tentative, exploratory walk revealed the city to be built on a network of stagnant, liquorice-smelling drains and canals choked with rubbish. Floating belly up in one of them was an enormous, bloated rat. Molly was shocked. Later that morning she walked with her measured, schoolmistress tread to the sea wall and looked out over the pink metallic sea to where she supposed England was. One of these two countries is imaginary, she thought. And I think it is this one.

Donella posed in the doorway. Behind her the ebony-faced maid did not look up as she dusted assiduously and moved things round the table.

'My dear, would you be so kind as to pass me my cigarettes? Please understand that you have caught me in a state of dire confusion because of this break-in. Maxine! Bring me some matches please.' The maid brought matches. 'I shall repair to my dressing-room and find some clothes to throw on my body after I have showered. In England, you know, I would shower however cold it was, whatever parts of me were freezing and dropping off. If I remember correctly, the English do not cleanse themselves too frequently.' She went off into some other part of the house.

The timbers of the verandah creaked, momentarily giving Molly the impression that she was on the deck of a huge white ship that sailed on dry land, going nowhere. She shook her head to dispel the sense of unreality, rose from her chair and walked to the end of the verandah where Maxine was sweeping. Stinking foul water from the narrow concrete trench running alongside the road made her stomach queasy. Molly attempted to catch Maxine's eye and smile. The maid steadfastly ignored her.

Something was approaching down the street. Molly blinked. At first sight it looked like a walking tree. She looked again. It was a man, thin and black, dressed entirely in shreds and tatters of cloth that had turned as black as his skin with age, sweat and heat. His hair grew knotted and wild. He walked with obsessive regularity of stride, stiff-legged as if his legs were branches hung with fluttering scraps of material. Barefoot, he progressed with astonishing speed, eyes fixed straight ahead.

'Who is this, Maxine?'

Maxine looked up indifferently from her broom and glanced down the street:

'The King of Rags.' She chewed on a matchstick.

'What does he do?' asked Molly.

'Me na know. 'E jus' walk.'

Maxine was still sulking over Donella's accusations that she had left the door unlocked. She swept on methodically, then added with a grin: 'Maybe he's walking for summady.'

'How do you mean?' Molly wondered if she meant he was going on an errand.

'Maybe he tryin' to walk summady to death.' She squinted at Molly in the sunlight. 'We can do that here, yuh know. 'I'll walk for you.' She shook her finger, indicating a mock threat, and laughed.

Donella reappeared dressed in a pair of light grey slacks and an expensively tailored blouse. Maxine served her breakfast outside:

'Excuse me eating my breakfast, dear. I figure you've already had yours.'

'That's all right,' said Molly with martyrish restraint. She watched Donella tuck into a plate of scrambled egg and tomato. Some of the food fell from her mouth onto the table:

'You know, when I was in England I was very friendly with the Duke of Blenheim's family. His cousin was a very good friend of mine. Do you know them at all?'

'I'm afraid not. They're a little out of my sphere,' replied Molly smugly.

Donella rattled on: 'Yes. She came to visit me in the clinic when my son was born – so drunk my dear, she was falling all over the room begging me to let her hold the baby and I was saying 'No . . . er . . . please don't.' I dare say if I was back there now she would be expecting me to sweep her floors.' She wiped her mouth on one of the paper napkins torn in quarters to make them last longer:

'You leave that country and nobody gives a squot!' she added bitterly.

The door buzzer sounded. A second or two later, Ralph Rawlings walked across the wide varnished floor to greet them. He was a bulky, balding mulatto of about forty-five with a loud shirt and squeaky shoes. He constantly adusted the black-rimmed spectacles on his nose:

'Some kinda chicken riot downtown.' Ralph always sounded exasperated, impatient. Now he was feeling especially burdened by this white stranger who had been foisted on him by his far-distant sister and to whom he had to play host.

'What kind of riot?' Donella exaggerated a mild panic. 'I am supposed to be doing a little supervision for someone downtown this morning.'

'Seemingly some chicken arrived from the States at half the normal price. People fightin' over it. It's the distribution that's all wrong in this blasted country. Distribution all the time.'

'I shall phone the shop immediately and tell them I am too distraught to undertake any supervision today. The loss of both the radio and the iron is catastrophic. I shall seize this opportunity to fly up to the Rupununi. I have been trying to organise a flight up there for days. Now, Ralph, might I prevail upon you to drive me to the airport? My car is out of commission until a new clutch flies in from Miami. My bag is packed and ready.' She clapped her hands with girlish eagerness.

Ralph looked at his watch. He could spare a couple of hours and Donella was useful to him. She had good contacts in transportation and knew of outlets for his timber business:

'How do you feel about comin' out to the airport?' he asked Molly.

'Well, it was on my schedule this morning to go down and buy some books and materials for my class . . .'

Donella interrupted. 'Don't be foolish my dear. All those books come from England. You can get them when you return. Besides, there's little enough here without you walking off with half the literature in the country.'

Molly did not attempt to argue.

The road to the airport was long and straight. Molly was bounced up and down on the broken springs of the back seat. Now and then she glimpsed the brown Demerara river through the bush. Donella addressed her from the front seat:

'You see, Molly, I have a dear friend, my alter ego, who is stranded up on her ranch in the Rupununi. She has nothing to eat, literally nothing but farine. She is relying on me. The herd got rabies. They're inoculated now but there will be no animals to sell for three months. The situation is utterly parlous.'

Donella turned to Ralph: 'Eight gallons of latex has come into my possession. What sort of price would you give me for it?'

The two of them bargained fiercely over the price.

Molly gripped the window frame and looked out. A small, dark, skinny man, one foot on the pedal of his bike, came scooting towards them along the grass verge at the side of the road. As the car neared him, she heard him bringing up the phlegm from the back of his throat. The gob of spittle hit her full in the forehead. Quickly, she retreated into the back of the car and took a handkerchief from her handbag. She wiped her face and then surreptitiously threw the handkerchief from the car window. Not surprising, she thought, given the history of the place, that someone should spit at a white face. Her own magnanimity and understanding of the incident warmed her. The others were still discussing the latex and hadn't noticed anything. After a while, Ralph stopped the car and bought three slices of fresh pineapple, cut lengthwise, from a sharp-eyed Indian woman at the side of the road. Molly remained in the back of the car, smiling. She gets on my nerves, thought Ralph, as he returned to the driving seat.

They walked through the airport which was in chaos. The air-conditioning had broken. A throng of people besieged the solitary man behind the check-in counter. Hands waved tickets and immigration papers in the air to attract his attention. Some passengers near the counter sat on their bags and refused to move although their flight had been cancelled. Ralph steered Molly towards a gap in the crowd. A disconsolate group stood round the telephone watching a man bang the receiver up and down trying to make it work. Donella went off to try and organise her flight. Molly suppressed her distaste at the general mêlée.

'Excuse me, Ralph,' she said. 'I have to use the toilet.'

She pushed her way through the crowded concourse wishing she had been able to keep to her original plan of browsing through the bookshop. The disorder upset her. A foul stench hit her as she entered the Ladies. She held her breath and entered one of the cubicles. The toilet was packed with shit. So was the next one. And the next. She exited quickly and drew breath:

'It's not very nice in there,' she said, apologetically.

'They should do something about this place,' said Ralph, darkly.

They went up the stairs to the bar. It was gloomy but not as crowded as outside. A black girl in a green and white check overall drooped lethargically behind the counter:

'We gat a power outage,' she said. 'We ain' gat no cold drinks. We gat carbonated orange and black cherry drink.' She wiped the bar down with a piece of paper. Ralph ordered a vodka and black cherry. Molly sipped an orange drink she did not want. She felt sick.

'See that man over there,' said Ralph. 'That's the Minister of Sport. They say his heart is not well. He should lose weight.' Molly turned to see a group of Afro-Guyanese men standing in the corner of the room laughing and drinking. The Minister laughed too but he looked anxious all the same. His eyes kept flicking from side to side as if there might be an enemy in the bar.

'Ralph Rawlings!'

A smartly dressed Malaysian woman with neatly permed black hair and a little button of a mouth held out her arms to Ralph. Her red linen suit made a splash of colour in the darkened bar-room. Molly made an effort to smile as she waited to be introduced.

'Mrs Chan. How you do? Meet Molly Summers, a visitor from England.'

A brief handshake and Mrs Chan turned back to Ralph:

'Well,' she sighed, 'I had to come back. I thought I was settled in Miami for good but I re-married to a Guyanese and I had to come back.' She looked around her and a shadow of disgust passed over her face. She caught Molly looking at her:

'My sons stayed behind though,' she added with pride. 'I jus' goin' back to see them now.'

She lowered her voice so that it was just audible over the hubbub of the bar:

'Joan Robson is back too.' She spoke with malicious satisfaction. 'See her over there. Remember how glamorous she used to be? Something happened. She was at Columbia University. Some story . . . racism . . . something dreadful happened. A suicide . . . something. There was a car crash too. See the scars on her face.'

Molly studied the slim, honey-coloured woman seated at a table nearby. The skin on her fine-boned face was discoloured in patches. Skin grafts.

'She used to be so beautiful!' continued Mrs Chan with barely suppressed glee. 'Her body lookin' old now. There was some kinda breakdown. Cocaine too, I heard. She looks like some kinda rehabilitated person, don't you think?'

Grim pleasure shone out of Mrs Chan's black eyes:

'Anyway. She back too. Marketing peppers. Which reminds me, Ralph. You wan' buy some cement? I can deal with the freight but not the duty. I can't handle the duty at all. I'll call you when I get back. Think about it. Well, I suppose I better go wiggle my behind at those immigration people.'

Ralph shook his head as he watched her weaving her way out through the waiting passengers:

'Is women doin' all the business now,' he said, as if he too experienced the indefinable turmoil that was affecting Molly.

A cheer went up at the arrival of some long-awaited flight from Trinidad. Two dark patches of sweat showed under the arms of Ralph's shirt and now he was arguing with the girl behind the bar. She had accidentally served him with pure water from a bottle instead of vodka. She was convulsed with laughter at her mistake.

The heavily pregnant black woman with close-cropped hair who had been observing Molly grasped her opportunity and glided across to stand directly in front of her. Molly had to bend her head to hear what she was saying:

'You can spare me a dollar, please?' Her big belly made the woman's dress ride up at the front and dip at the back, like a child's. She spoke quietly. Molly reached in her purse and willingly handed over three dollars. The woman took it and vanished. The dark room bubbled with conversation. Molly had the sensation that she was under water. Unable to breathe freely. She shut her eyes and tried to focus on the purpose of her visit. Donella's high-pitched voice cut through the noise:

'I am in despair.' She faced them, arms akimbo. 'No flights. Freddie has to wait for a consignment of something that is stuck in Customs. It's too disastrous. My alter ego will starve.'

The three of them trailed across the airport car park: Donella wringing her hands and lamenting, Ralph perspiring heavily, Molly tip-toeing behind because the tarmac was burning the soles of her feet even through the sandals. A savage, unremitting heat replaced the swirling confusion of the airport. Molly felt that she had turned into a mirage, shimmering and unreal. The ground radiated heat. She pulled the top of her soaking blue cotton dress away from her breasts before getting into the back of the car. The seat scorched her thighs. She felt dizzy.

'Your car still gat four tyres, sir. I guardin' it for you.'

Ralph gave the urchin some coins and clambered into the driving seat. Molly leaned back weakly as they set off. Her thoughts were becoming disjointed. She was unable to concentrate on anything. She closed her eyes then opened them briefly and saw an endless expanse of blue sky with two clouds like white meringues. The black speck of a vulture hovered over the bush in the distance. She closed her eyes once more. Too much sky, she thought. On the journey back, pictures swam behind her eyelids; the pregnant beggar woman teaching a class in her school in London; Maxine, the maid, casually chewing on a match as she examined a rack of shoes in the shop at Finsbury Park. They reached town. Ralph drove past Stabroek market towards the Chase Manhattan bank. Molly spotted the King of Rags, stationary now, standing near a pile of dried-out coconut trash talking to a man with a tray of watches for sale. Ralph pulled over by the bank. People streamed from the pavement round the car. Molly tried to suppress a feeling of dislike for the throng of unfamilar faces; mahogany faces, cinnamon faces, ebony faces, agate faces. She yearned for the cool peace of the Meeting House.

So swiftly did the figure move to her side of the car that Molly barely had time to register it. For a second or two glaring sun prevented her from seeing that it was the figure of a white man, not more than twenty-five years old. Rough, unshaven stubble glittered ginger on the bottom half of his face as he thrust it in through the car window. The hair was cropped short in a crew-cut that could have belonged to a soldier or a convict. The face reddened by exposure to the sun made his blue eyes look fierce. He was blinking as he leaned in towards Molly:

'Are you English?' The accent was cockney.

'Yes.' Molly's pale forehead puckered with astonishment.

'Gimme some money,' he whined menacingly.

She stared at him in disbelief.

'Gimme some money. I want some dinner.'

She made a feeble attempt to wind up the window but the mechanism was broken. He persisted:

'I was in Pentonville prison. D'you know it? Near Kings Cross.'

She nodded dumbly. He shoved his head further in the car and she pulled her head back into a nest of chins. He continued:

'I used to live in Streatham Hill. D'you know round there?'

She nodded again, speechless, her mouth dry. His foot slipped on some garbage in the gutter and he stepped back. She saw his plimsolls dirty and without laces; the jeans ragged at the bottom; his navy-blue vest torn and stained. She raised her eyes. He seemed enormous. His head eclipsed the sun, a fiery halo dancing round its silhouette, the sky stretching away behind.

'My wife left me. I had a nervous breakdown. That's when they put me in Pentonville. Dr Rhodes sent me here. You must have heard of Dr Rhodes. He sent me here. He sent me here.'

The voice was echoing in Molly's ears.

'Help me. I must get back. I'm tryin' to get me fare back.'

'But . . . but,' Molly stammered, 'you're English. You shouldn't be doing this.'

Something was happening to her. The sun seemed to have broken loose from its moorings and to be moving round in circles in the sky. She heard the voice faintly now:

'Well just give me the money for me dinner. I'm starvin'.'

Ralph came out of the bank. He pushed the man out of the

way and got into the car. Molly was making little whimpering sounds in the back.

'Girl – you all right?' he asked anxiously.

'He's English . . . that beggar . . . a white man.'

She became aware of Donella and Ralph looking over their shoulders at her curiously. Suddenly an enormous rage consumed the whole of her body as if somehow or other she had been tricked. She tried to speak but no words came. Ralph saw that she was gasping for breath and noticed little purple blotches appearing on her face. She tried to correct her mistake. What she wanted to say was perfectly clear in her head and it would make everything all right again. It would stop the doubtful accusing looks on the faces of those two people staring at her from the front seats. But her lips just moved without producing a sound like a fish out of water. Slumped against the back seat she started to gurgle. Her grey hair was soaked with sweat. A small child poked at her through the window trying to sell her some peanuts.

'Blast it,' thought Ralph. 'Don' tell me the woman has come all the way over here just to die in the back of my car.' He started up the engine and headed for the Public Hospital.

THE CONVERSION
OF MILLICENT VERNON

In the distance, the bell from the Lutheran church started to sound. A minute or so later it was joined by the lugubrious, deeper bell of the Anglican church. For a while these two bells limped along together, out of step, and then the high sweet chimes of the Catholic church rang out, intermingling with them and confusing the difference between all three.

Millicent Vernon, a light-skinned girl of eighteen leaned her elbows on the rail of Canje Bridge and stared dejectedly into the brown creek waters. Selma, her friend, stood with her back to the rail jutting out her pointy breasts like an old poster of Jane Russell she had once seen and spitting the stones from purply-black jamoon fruit into the road.

'Oh God, Selma, is how I goin' get money to fix me teeth?'

'Write your cousin in England and beg her the money. You know how we Guyanese like to beg.' Selma gave a malicious smile.

The two girls turned and began to stroll back to New Amsterdam. A carload of boys in an ancient jalopy passed them, whooping and hollering in the early evening light. Selma threw them one of her sultry, haughty looks as she strutted along in her skin-tight, shiny blue pants, slapping at the sandflies as they bit. Millie wore a white blouse and red shorts. Her long legs turned to gold in the evening sunlight. Somewhere, in the bush alongside the creek, a keskidee bird was calling.

On their right, set back off the road in a patch of land that seemed a wilderness, stood the rambling ramshackle madhouse. From one of the upper storeys, as they passed, came the sound of a woman's voice screaming like a cat:

'Bring me someting, please. Bring me someting, please.'

The girls shrieked and ran.

It was dusk as the two girls walked into the centre of town. People stood in knots outside in the warm night air, lounging against the wall of a rum shop, liming, passing the time of day. Flambeaux, lit by the street-vendors, flickered on trestle tables lighting the meagre range of buns and peanuts and sweets. It was a ghost town in more ways than one. In this place the ghosts walked openly and brazenly in the streets. The blue eyes of a Dutch planter looked enquiringly out of the black face of the local midwife; the wrists of an Indian indentured labourer who had died a hundred years earlier were the same wrists that twisted brown paper round the peanuts Millie bought at the stall. Mr Chan's face had skipped down the centuries, travelling through Demerara and all the way to Panama and back before arriving to peer anxiously from the doorway of his restaurant on this, the main thoroughfare of New Amsterdam. With each decade the genetic kaleidoscope shifted and a greater variety of ghosts appeared, sometimes as many as four or five mischievously occupying one body. Jumbie people. That is the best way of describing the population of New Amsterdam, capital of Berbice county. Jumbie people.

There had been no electricity for four weeks. Apart from Mr Chan's restaurant which had its own generator, the only illumination in the street came from the pots of fire on the vendors' tables, an unstable flickering light that cast weird shadows on the moving faces. Millie was trying to dislodge the crunched peanuts from the cavities in her back teeth when Selma whispered in her ear:

'See Mrs Singh over there?' Millie glanced at the full bosomed Indian woman examining sandals at a stall. Selma continued:

'She can't get children.' Selma's eyes were small, hard and black as ackee seeds. 'They say that after she marry, her pussy stop being sweet and creamy an' it start to spout ammonia and acids. Then it start to talk an' say rude tings an' her husband too frighten to go near her.'

At that moment, Mrs Singh looked up straight into Millie's eyes. Millie felt herself flushing.

'Good evening, Millie.' She called across. 'Say hello to your mother for me.'

'Yes, tank you, Mrs Singh.'

Selma continued relentlessly:

'Anyway, her husband send her to see an Indian obeah man and he tell her she must take an image of Mother Cathari – that's the evil one of seven Indian sisters – and keep it under her pillow and then her pussy will stop talkin' and spittin' poisons and she can get children.'

'Shhhhhh. Selma you wicked.' Millie looked troubled. Her mother had tried to stop her seeing too much of Selma but as she lived next door, it was impossible. When Millie asked why, her mother had replied grimly:

'Because that girl don' give satisfaction, that's why.'

Millie and Selma walked in silence to New Street where they lived.

'Bye, Selma.' Selma climbed gingerly the disintegrating wooden steps of the one-storey house on stilts. When she reached the top she turned and waved like a film star on the steps of an airplane, before vanishing into the dark, rotting timber jaws of the house.

Millie hung around on the steps of her own house. How could she tell her mother that she needed one hundred and fifty dollars to save her teeth? She went in. Her mother bent over the sewing machine working by the light of the kerosene lamp. Granny slept in one of the threadbare armchairs, her bad leg thick and swollen like a turtle's leg resting on a stool.

'Millie, quick, come watch this rice for me while I fetch the washing.' Christine, her sister, stood by the stove in a loose blue tee-shirt and brown corduroy pants. She sniffed under her arm:

'Phew! I'm rank,' she said. Her four-year-old daughter, Joanne, chattered at her side. Christine bent over to fasten the child's ribbon:

'If you lose this ribbon you can't get another and it's no more party time. Understand?'

Millie poked at the rice to stop it catching at the bottom of the pan. She turned to tell Christine what the dentist had said about her teeth but Christine had already disappeared down the back steps into the yard. A minute or two later she returned, arms full of washing, prattling in her shrill voice:

'Well, Millie girl, they tell me at work today that another one of that family in Fyrish drop down dead. That makes twelve altogether. You know how it start?'

Millie took the boiling corn off the stove and put the curry back on the burner. She shook her head disinterestedly at the question. Christine was the only one of the family with work – as a clerk in the bauxite factory:

'Well. This boy in Fyrish left his girlfriend with their baby and went away to Miami. When he came back he say that he goin' marry another girl an' he call this new girl his fiancée. The baby-mother sent this new fiancée a custard block and soon she dead. Then the boy dead. At first they think is the girl do it. Then she dead too. All the family keep dying. They call in a big obeah man – the very best from Surinam. They call him Jucka. Whatever it is he do, it can't work. Cousins, aunties, one by one they keep dying. A policeman try to call at the house but when he reach the door he start shakin' and he turn and run. The house is empty. Fowls and goats left to run loose. Nobody enters.' Christine had taken over from Millie's half-hearted efforts at the stove and was banging pots and shifting the steaming pans onto the sideboard as she spoke:

'Now they say is Bakoo do it.'

'What's a Bakoo, Mummy?' enquired Joanne.

'It's a thing they keep in a bottle,' replied Christine, warning Millie with a look that the conversation should stop.

The meal was served. Millie's two elder brothers emerged from the back bedroom which they shared. Mrs Vernon took her place at the head of the table. Behind her head on the blue-painted wooden wall hung an anaemic picture of Christ. Strung below that on a nylon thread was a row of faded Christmas and birthday cards. Mrs Vernon said grace. The family bent their heads:

'For what we are about to receive, may the Lord make us truly thankful. Amen.'

The meal consisted of half a piece of bad corn each. Rice. Curry without meat. Some pieces of black pudding. A salad made from tomatoes and cucumber. Millie toyed with her corn.

Just as she was about to mention her teeth, Mrs Vernon started up in her twittering voice:

'That sewing machine can't mend. The timing belt is gone. The Lord knows what will happen. The council has written to say if we don't pay the back taxes on the house they goin' put it up for sale. Fitzpatrick, Colin, you must go to Georgetown in the morning and look for work there if you can't find it here. You can stay with Uncle Freddie.'

'Don' fret. We find the money somewhere.' Colin was always full of empty promises.

'Joanne,' Christine lifted her daughter down from the stool, 'run to the Chinee and beg a piece of ice for Granny's drink.'

Millie left the table. She took a candle and went to inspect her teeth in the cubicle that passed for a bathroom. Inside, there was a corroded tin bath and an ancient cranky shower attachment. No water. The water in the town had been turned off for nearly three weeks apart from the standpipe in the back yard. People put out pots and pans to catch water when it rained. Millie wrinkled her nose at the sour stench. She took the piece of broken mirror from the ledge and examined her teeth. In the uneven light from the candle she could just see the holes in the bottom back teeth. More serious was a brown patch, the beginning of a cavity in one of her top teeth right at the front. She felt sick. She practised smiling without showing her teeth. Underneath her feet, a hole in the floorboards allowed a glimpse of the ground below. Avoiding it, she slipped through the back way into the kitchen, scooped a cup of water from the big pan and returned to the bathroom to scrub her teeth obsessively. There was no toothpaste. Toothpaste and soap were in short supply in New Amsterdam.

The boys had dissolved into the dark night. The family sat in the living area lit by the kerosene lamp. Four wooden pillars supported the sloping eaves of the house. Pictures of Christ adorned the walls. The nylon curtains tied with plastic hair-bows hung still in the airless night. Nobody spoke. Christine was dabbing methylated spirits on Joanne's mosquito bites. Millie hoicked her legs over the arm of the chair. She could wait no longer. Her voice was croaky:

'Mummy, I went to the dentist today and he say I goin' lose

my teeth unless I can give him one hundred and fifty dollars to save them.'

Mrs Vernon frowned:

'Oh dear, oh lor'. Millie, I don' know what you goin' do. All I can think you must do is go to church and pray and by the grace of God, He will help you. I can' help you.'

Millie wished she'd never asked.

'That's all right, Mummy. I goin' write to Evangeline to see if she can send the money.'

'If you write to Evangeline,' said her mother, 'ask her please if she could send me a timing belt with thirty-five links for a Singer sewing machine, model 319.'

That night, Millie could not sleep. She shared her bed with her mother. Her tossing and turning eventually obliged Mrs Vernon to get up and sprinkle her with holy water to let her sleep. In the morning, the sound of her mother sweeping woke her. Quickly, she dressed, plaited her hair and hung the mosquito net on the nail in the rafter overhead. Then she fetched a pen and paper and sat on the edge of the bed. The floorboards felt warm under her toes. She puckered her forehead and bit the end of the pen, staring unseeingly at the socks and panties hung on a wire across one corner of the room. Then she began:

17 January, 1987

My dear cousin Evangeline,

How are you? I do hope this letter reaches yourself in the pink of health. As for me I'm fine.

Evangeline, as you know I am not working yet and things are very tough in the home at present. Evangeline, I would be very thankful if you could send me some money to get my teeth done. My teeth has started to decay. I would be glad if you could send whatever you could afford. I know you would understand the situation, if I delay until next year I would lose my teeth completely, for when I went for the examination of my teeth the dentist told me, by the next two months if I don't fill them I would lose them. I would hate to lose them.

Do you remember I told you I was waiting on my advanced typewriting results? I was successful but there is no jobs.

Evangeline, I am enclosing a dollar bill wrapped in carbon paper to give you an idea how to post the money.

It cannot be detected that way.

Care yourself, I would always remember you in my prayers.

Your loving cousin, Millie.

P.S. Please send mummy a timing belt (35 links) for a 319 Singer machine.

After she had dropped Joanne off at school, Millie ran back down Main Street and cut up through King Street to the Strand, her thick plaited pony-tail leaping and flying behind her. The morning sun was extraordinarily bright, its corona dancing in circles. As yet there was not much heat. She flew past clumps of banana trees that leaned their tattered leaves over fences like common gossips. She posted the letter, turned round and bumped slap into Mad Max Marks:

'Poop me loops, sister Millie.' The mulatto's green eyes sauntered lasciviously down her slim body and up again to her neck. 'That's a pretty necklace.' Millie's hands leapt up to where her blue necklace was fastened at the back:

'How much will you give me for it?' He scratched his ginger hair:

'Three dollar. Pity it ain' green. Green is obeah colour. People pay more for green.'

She gave him the necklace and put the money down the front of her blouse. It's a start, she thought, for my teeth money.

Millie rounded the corner of New Street. Outside her house two women were arguing. One of them was Selma's mother. A small group had gathered to watch as the two women circled each other in the yard:

'Yuh lie! Yuh mad! If you lay one finger on my chile again I goin' box you upside down.'

'Is your chile put grease on the wall,' screamed Selma's mother, 'an' it spoil my pants. I give him one big lick an' he deserve it.'

'That wall is 'e father's property. 'E can do what 'e like with it. 'E put grease there to stop you sittin' an' limin' 'pon it.'

' 'E's a dutty little scunt.'

Before they could exchange blows, Selma's eleven-year-old brother shot out of their house calling for his mother:

'Mummy come, quick quick. Sometin' happenin' to Selma.'

Selma's mother spat at the neighbour, tossed her black curls and waddled as fast as she could up the stairs and into the house.

'Wha'appenin', Jonjo?' Millie was curious. The boy's eyes had widened with fright:

'Selma catch some kinda fit. She on the floor wrigglin' like a bushmaster snake an' she can just grunt. An' a whole heapa spit comin' outta she mouth.' He ran back in the house.

Millie could hear muffled thumps from inside. Seconds later he re-emerged taking a flying leap down the stairs and swerving to avoid Millie. Without stopping he shouted:

'Mummy says I must fetch Mr Evans from the Backdam.'

Apprehensively, Millie watched his bare heels kicking up behind him as he ran. Mr Evans was an obeah man. She trailed up the stairs to her house, part of her wanting to stay outside and see what went on, part of her frightened by it. In the cool, dark interior, Mrs Vernon was fixing her hat ready for a church meeting. She had heard Jonjo's shouted remark:

'Millie, don' business with those people. They deal with their troubles their own way. We is Catholics remember.'

'What does that mean, exactly?' Millie asked, truculently.

Mrs Vernon looked nonplussed:

'It means we go forth and do the best we can,' she said vaguely. 'Come to church with me now to say some prayers and maybe God will help you.'

'No tanks, Mummy. My throat is hurtin' me. I stay here.'

Mrs Vernon descended the stairs. Her small head poking out of the big frilled collar of her dress and her springy step made her look like a turkey.

Millie went into the kitchen and cut a piece of cornmeal pone. Then she took up position in her bedroom and watched from the window.

Shortly, Mr Evans appeared marching purposefully towards

Selma's house. He was a short, stocky black man of about forty, his dark suit buttoned up at the front despite the heat. His white shirt bit into his thick neck. Under one arm he carried a briefcase, like an accountant. Behind him, Jonjo hopped nervously from side to side as if he were herding a great bull up the street. Millie knelt on the bed to see them enter the house. The door slammed shut behind them.

Millie explored her teeth with her tongue. If Mr Evans was as powerful as people said, perhaps she should ask him for help. She wondered how much he charged. Then she slipped off the bed and opened the ill-fitting bottom drawer of the chest quietly so Granny wouldn't wake. In a cardboard box at the back were several hundred dollars saved by her mother to pay back taxes on the house. Five thousand were owing altogether. Millie took out fifty and stuffed them down the front of her blouse. The room was hot and stuffy. For a while she sat on the bed staring into space. Then she heard a noise. She looked out of the window to see Jonjo being sick over the side of his steps. She ran down and beckoned to him from the shadows of her own bottom-house:

'Pssst. Jonjo. Wha 'appenin' in there?' Jonjo looked subdued as he approached wiping his mouth with the back of his hand:

'Mr Evan took a spirit out of Selma.'

'Did you see him do it?' The boy nodded and came and crouched on the ground in the shade under Millie's house. He started to describe what had happened in a monotonous little voice:

'First he did light a sulphur candle. Then 'e lock the door and block up the key-hole with a rag. Then 'e look for all the cracks in the windows and block them up too. All the time, Selma gruntin' like a hog in a cart.'

Millie tried to imagine Selma like that – Selma, who always managed somehow to emerge from that black pit of a house immaculately turned out, smart as paint. Jonjo continued:

'Then he put healin' oil on she hair and knotted the hair so the bad spirit can' get out that way. 'E pour oil in she ears too. Then 'e question the spirit an' ask it why it troublin' Selma. Thas when I start feel sick but they wouldn't let me open the door and come out in case it got out with me. So I jus' sit under the table an' cover me eyes wid me hands. When I peep out, 'e holdin' a bottle to Selma's ear. 'E said some things and call the spirit into the bottle an' Selma start to jerk. Then 'e put the stopper on the bottle. Thas when they let me out. I hear him tell Mummy 'e goin' put it in cement and throw it in the river.'

'How is Selma?' Millie needed to know for sure if this business worked.

'All right. I tink she sleepin'.'

Jonjo wandered off a little dazed. Millie waited nervously for Mr Evans to come out. It was mid-day. The heat was unbearable. Not many people were out. Eventually, the door of Selma's house opened just long enough to let Mr Evans out before banging shut again. He paused to wipe his brow and the back of his neck with a white handkerchief, then set off down the street. Millie followed him. Across Main Street. Past the church. Up Crab Street and through a network of little streets that led down to the Backdam. Once or twice Millie tried to call out to him but her voice wouldn't work.

He lived at the end of a row of old slave logies on the Backdam. She did not want to enter the house. People said the walls were covered in chicken blood and the tap dripped human blood. As he reached his front door, Millie managed to call out:

'Mr Evans.' He turned. 'Mr Evans, can you help me please?'

'Come in, chile.' He went in through the door. She had no choice but to follow him.

The tiny room was spotlessly clean and neat as a pin. From an armchair in the corner an old black woman, smoking a clay pipe, nodded and smiled. Mr Evans put down his briefcase, lowered himself into the other armchair and leaned back expansively like a bank manager greeting a client:

'What can I do for you?' Millie's lips felt dry and split:

'I ain' havin' no luck an' me teeth need to fix. I gat fifty-three dollars. Can you help me, please?' Her voice sounded like a goat bleating. He regarded the young girl, beads of sweat on her upper lip:

'You tink someone is doin' you harm?'

'I don' know,' said Millie miserably.

He rose suddenly and went over to a small cupboard. Out of the cupboard he took four eggs intricately tied with black thread:

'I tell you what you must do. See these eggs? Put these eggs under where you sleep tonight and bring them back to me in the morning. That way we find out someting.' He pocketed the money Millie offered and muttered a polite goodbye.

Excitedly, she picked her way past the sluggish waters of the Backdam, holding the eggs carefully.

That night, after dark, she crept down and placed the four eggs by the timber post directly under her bedroom. She glanced over at Selma's house. It was ominously quiet. She covered the eggs with an upturned colander so that no animal could get at them and placed a tin can on top of the colander so that she would hear the noise if somebody tried to move it. In the morning she was up, dressed and out before her mother had stirred. The eggs were still there.

Mr Evans was yawning and rubbing the sleep from his eyes as he took the eggs from Millie. There was no sign of the old woman. He broke the eggs one at a time into a shiny aluminium pot. In each egg there shone a glistening sharp needle. Mr Evans pointed them out to Millie:

'Someone put these under where you sleep to do you harm. The eggs has sucked them up in the night. Your luck will change up now.'

Millie hovered in the doorway. It didn't seem enough. She wanted him to do something more. Sensing her dissatisfaction, he added: 'One more ting. Next time you pass a Congo pump tree – mek sure seh you touch it. Lay your hands 'pon it. Wish and pray to it. Good mornin'.'

Millie returned home with a feeling of anti-climax in her stomach. Her teeth were no nearer being fixed and she had taken her mother's money and spent it. Over the next few days she had a gnawing fear that her mother would count the money and find some missing. She became irritable and grumpy. She kept examining her teeth in the mirror. One day she met Jonjo in the street and asked him about Selma.

'She OK now. 'Cept she don' speak no more.'

Millie fretted and fretted. Finally, she went down with a full-blown fever. Her throat was painful and swollen. Her mother fluttered over her with prayers and rubbed her neck with camphorated oil at night. Over a fortnight passed.

On the first day that she felt properly well, Millie sat out on the front steps. It was cloudy. She was still weak. Her mother brought her out a warm cherry drink and some pieces of sugar cane stripped and cut in three-inch lengths. She bit into the woody stem and sucked the sweet juice letting it run down the back of her throat. At first she did not see it. A piece of tooth sticking in the sugar cane. Then she gave a cry and put her hand to her mouth. She picked out the piece of jagged tooth, dashed the plate away and ran to the mirror with her hand still over her mouth. What she saw was like looking into the gates of hell itself. There was a gaping black hole where half her front tooth had come away.

She was running. Down Main Street. Past King Street. Out of the town. Somewhere where nobody could see her. The bush. She wanted to hide deep in the bush, pull it round her. Thunder rumbled over the creek. A short burst of rain made her shelter under the wooden porch of a house. Then she was running again. Instead of going over Canje Bridge, she plunged down the banks towards the creek itself. Crying now, she stumbled along the muddy tracks by Canje Creek. Turkey grass and razor grass slashed at her legs. The piece of tooth remained clenched in her fist.

She came to an enclosed patch of land, bound on one side by the creek and on the other three sides by a tangle of tall bushes, bamboo, cane and wild eddoe plants. Someone had set fire to it to clear the land for planting. Everything was charred and burnt. The blackened stumps of one or two trees stuck up out of the scorched trash on the ground, a burnt mess of coconut leaves and awara tree leaves; a desolate, incinerated place. Millie flopped down on a boulder. After a while the crying stopped, leaving a dull sensation of misery. She stared at her wet brown feet in their flip-flop sandals. The luminous orange nail varnish that someone had told her punks wore in England was flaking off her toes. She bent down and fingered the leaves of a sleep-and-wake plant that had sprung up by the boulder. The leaves curled up slowly as she touched them. The massy protuberance on the tree trunk next to her was an ants' nest, so she moved to another rock. There she stayed, motionless, head bowed. An hour passed. Tree-frogs were croaking after the rain. Raindrops glistened on the wild eddoes. Slowly, the sun travelled across the sky, gleaming balefully now and then from behind great grey clouds. A chicken-hawk flew down onto one of the burnt tree stumps. It surveyed the scene, turning its head sharply this way and that, then flapped off over the bushes.

It began to grow dark. The waters of Canje Creek turned a glittering black. Millie shivered at a gust of wind. She got up slowly like someone stiff with rheumatism. Putting the fragment of tooth in her pocket, she bent and plucked some black sage to use as soap. She crushed it in her hand and trod through the marshy undergrowth at the creek's edge. There, she freshened her hands with the soapy substance from the plant and rinsed her face and hands with creek water. As she turned to clamber back, she looked up and drew in her breath with a gasp.

On the opposite side of the patch of land stood a gigantic Congo pump tree, its black silhouette outlined sharply against a moving backdrop of grey clouds. The tapering trunk lacked all foliage until the very top where the branches splayed out flat as a pancake. Mesmerised by the sight, Millie's eyes remained fixed on the magnificent, stately tree. It was without doubt the king of trees, ancient and powerful. It was as though it had sprung up behind her while her back was turned at the creek. Her heart was thumping. The wind rustled the bamboo and cane hedges as she ran across the burnt scrub to place her hands on the cool trunk. She bent her head back to look up once more at the top of the tree and went giddy at the dizzying height of it. Leaning her cheek against the trunk she prayed and wished for everything to come right. After two or three minutes, she fished the piece of tooth out of her pocket, scratched away some earth from the base of the tree and buried it.

Without a backward glance and feeling more at peace than she had for weeks, Millie left the patch of land and walked home.

Christine, hands on hips, waited for her at the top of the steps:

'Is where you been, Millie?' her shrill voice scolded. 'You din' pick up Joanne from school. Two hours she waitin' there. Mummy had to leave her church meetin' to fetch her an' the teacher sittin' there with a face like a squeezed lime.'

Millie opened her mouth and showed Christine the gap-tooth. Christine was shocked into silence and then remembered:

'Oh, there's a letter for you from England.'

Millie opened the letter and screamed with joy. Folded in carbon paper just as she had instructed were two United States twenty dollar bills, enough to pay the dentist's bill and replace her mother's money. She flung her arms round Christine, who reeked of onions, and they danced together on the greyish floorboards. In the bedroom doorway, Mrs Vernon stood smiling, flourishing a letter of her own:

'Praise the Lord,' she said. 'The timing belt is on its way.'

As Mrs Vernon said grace that evening, Millie cast a sly look up at the pale, impotent picture of Christ on the wall. She knew without a shadow of doubt that it was the Congo pump tree that had worked her good fortune. Mrs Vernon brought out the bottle of Banko that was kept for special occasions and proposed a toast thanking the Good Lord for their fortune. Millicent Vernon raised her glass and pledged her secret allegiance to the Congo pump tree.

A DISGUISED LAND

It was three years after Winsome arrived in England from Jamaica that the dream started to come. She was fourteen and the dream was always more or less the same.

She dreamed she was in England and that she had been sentenced to death. She appeared to be free, standing on the pavement outside a court somewhere in a country town. Small knots of white people stood chatting like parents after a school function. They were always extremely kind to her. In one of the dreams a man drew up beside her in his car. He put his head out of the window and said helpfully:

'Hop in and I'll give you a lift to the gallows. It's not far out of my way.' Winsome felt cold wet patches of sweat under the arms of her dress:

'No. I jus' walk there. Tank you.' Her fear seemed inappropriate amongst such pleasantly relaxed people. A taboo caught her tongue and forbade her to say how she felt. Sometimes a woman with two yappy dogs at her feet would apologise for the dogs' behaviour, as they bounced up at Winsome's legs, and then turn back to the conversation with her friends. In the dream Winsome was always dressed the way her grandmother used to dress when she went to church in Clarendon; a navy-blue straw hat pinned down on her springy hair, low-heeled shoes with no stockings, a pale blue crimplene dress, white gloves, and she clutched a navy-blue plastic handbag. The white people round her were dressed casually in loose blouses and skirts and sandals, making her feel over-dressed. On a wave of polite chit-chat she was carried inexorably to her execution, unable to protest, unable to shout, silenced by the informal friendliness of those who surrounded her. The dream had variations but the fact that she was to be killed never varied.

The last thing Mrs Hyacinth Nevins had wanted was for her daughter, Winsome, to come to England despite frequent sentimental references to the longed-for reunion with her first-born child. When the letter arrived with the Clarendon postmark, her heart sank. The spidery writing confirmed her fears. Her mother could no longer cope with Winsome and wanted to send her to England. The reality of her daughter's imminent arrival caused a mild fury to fizz up in her. She stood with the letter in her hand. She looked at the orange and black patterned carpet in the front room of her council flat. She inspected the glass-topped coffee table adorned with a profusion of acrylic crocheted doilies and she studied the glass-fronted cabinet crammed with china shepherdesses, little figurines and carefully arranged red glassware. Hardest of all she stared at the posed photograph of her three British children by Mr Maurice Nevins that rested on the mantelpiece over the gas fire. She bit her lip and tried to remember what Winsome looked like. All she could remember was a dark, sullen baby who squatted on her knee heavily like a bullfrog about to leap off and flop untidily in another part of the room. She went into her bedroom and sat on the pink candlewick bedspread.

'Jus' when we get on our feet,' she said out loud. Then she cussed. She cussed the day she had ever met Winsome's 'dyam no good fader'. She cussed her spindly-writing mother for becoming too frail to raise Winsome, and finally she cussed the dark lump of her own flesh who was about to descend on her life and disrupt it.

Years later, dressed to the nines, Winsome sat in the shabby offices of the Probation Service in Southwark. She was asked about her relationship with her mother. She remembered her mother yelling: 'Yuh too like yuh dyam no good fader. Stubborn little pickney.' She remembered her younger brother and sisters teasing her over her Jamaican accent and other children in the playground taunting her until, cornered in the playground by the drinking fountain, she had fought. She remembered telling her mother that she wanted to be a model and her mother crinkling up her eyelids, thick with lizard-green eyeshadow, and saying, 'Yuh ugly ting. Yuh too hugly!'

'My mum was OK, as it 'appens,' said Winsome, unsmiling, to the probation officer, or rather to the typewriter on the probation officer's desk which was where the answers seemed to be required. She felt a scornful distaste at the woman's dowdy clothes. Besides which, she looked like a praying mantis. She was thin, her elbows stuck out and her head was held on one side just like the insect. She had a dry and dusty smile as she said:

'I'm sure we can help you get over this little bad patch, dear.'

Winsome just wanted to get out of the office. She wanted to get back home to her kids.

Winsome's two little girls were two of the best-dressed kids in Laverna Court block. They wanted for nothing. And to see that they had everything and that the home was in good shape, Winsome went out kiting. Her boyfriend Junior Watson, baby-father of the two children, provided her with the cheque-books and cheque cards from which he had removed the signature with brake fluid, although the banks were beginning to cotton on to that and making it more difficult to do. In one altercation, Junior had also provided her with an ugly scar on her left upper lip from his switchblade, but Winsome was a big woman and strong and Junior was also left with a bump over his eyebrow that never quite disappeared. Sometimes he stayed the night with her but mostly he returned home to his mother in Shepherds Bush where there was more space. He wore a small diamond in his ear and drove a red Capri, so that was what his friends called him – Red Capri. Winsome's friend Sonia looked after the kids when Winsome went out to pass the cheques in shops and banks. Junior also provided Winsome with her third pregnancy.

The dream came and went at intervals. Now it included references to the children. One time, the praying mantis detached herself from one of the groups outside the courthouse and approached Winsome, smiling:

'Don't worry, Winsome. We'll look after the children. I will explain to them that you had to be executed.' Winsome felt embarrassed as she tried to decline the offer:

'It's all right, thank you. My friend Sonia . . .'

'But we've got all the room in the world,' said the praying mantis.

Suddenly, Winsome's grandmother appeared, bible in hand, saying:

'How many times I haffi tell yuh. Don' speak with duppies!'

Winsome woke up in her Peckham flat. The children had crawled into bed and were asleep on her neck and chest, stifling her. No sign of Junior. She could hear the noise of the speakers still hissing in the front room. She heaved herself out of bed, put on a wrap and went to look. Levi, a lanky Rasta friend of Junior's, was asleep in a chair. She went to pull the curtains, accidentally treading on one of the full ashtrays on the brown carpet. Levi stirred and stretched.

'Where's Capri?' asked Winsome.

' 'Im gaan,' Levi yawned.

'You want some plantain and fish, Levi?'

'What kinda fish you gat?'

'Salt-fish.'

'Thas cool. Is mackerel me nah deal wid. De mackerel dem feed offa dead men.' He shuddered. Then he took off his tam and shook out his locks. As he began to reach down for the little packet of herb on the floor, two-year-old Chantale waddled through the doorway and began to pull on his locks and grab at the Rizla in his hand. He disentangled her gently.

Winsome went into the bathroom to wash and dress. Junior would probably not come back that day. She regarded her five-month pregnant belly in the mirror. It hardly showed. But she felt sluggish. In the kitchen she poked at the plantain and watched the oil turning a greenish colour in the pan. Levi lounged against the wall behind her:

'Is when you go back to de court, Winsome?' he enquired.

'The day before the baby is due, would you believe it? I don't think they'll do me nothing. Just a fine.' The plantain spat in the pan as she turned it over. 'I'll probably drop this one in the dock.'

'Yuh must watch yuhself in some of dem courts,' warned Levi. 'Especially the older courts. They gat certain magic writings on the walls to do harm to black people. Ancient spells fi mek us confuse when we stand in de dock deh.'

Winsome sucked her teeth and prodded at the salt-fish.

'Fi true,' he insisted. 'I see it myself one time. Writings on de wall an' yuh cyan understan' it. Babylon writings.' He took a piece of plantain from the pan with a fork and burnt his lips on it. 'I don' wait for de fish, Winsome, I gaan.' He piled his locks back into the tam and made for the front door. She watched him loping across the yard.

Later that day, after she had signed on at the dole office, Winsome stood in a branch of Mothercare fingering a little pair of white, kid-leather shoes. She held onto the shoes and flicked through a rack of baby smocks with green and yellow appliquéd rabbits on them. She collected up several pairs of blue and white baby-grows, then deftly removed the tags from everything and went up to the counter:

'Oh, excuse me. I bought these a couple of months ago when I was expecting and I lost the baby and I wondered if you could give me a refund?'

'Do you have the receipts?' asked the woman.

'No, I'm sorry,' Winsome summoned tears to her eyes. 'I was so upset at the time I don't know what I done with them.'

The woman behind the counter became embarrassed. There she sat in this temple of motherhood, this shrine to the pastel glories of maternity, laden with coats and baby pillows, crocheted bootees, festooned with little hanging mobiles, kiddies' duvets and tiny towelling all-in-ones, surrounded by bright plastic rattles, soft cuddly toys and disposable nappies. And here she was faced with this cumbersome black woman with a badly scarred lip, crying because she had had a miscarriage. She gave Winsome a sympathetic look and went to whisper something in the supervisor's ear. Returning quickly, she totted up the amount of the goods Winsome had handed her, reached into the till and gave Winsome the sum of thirty-eight pounds. As Winsome went to the door she felt the baby kicking inside her. She took a bus down the high street to another branch of Mothercare and paid for one or two items for the new baby. Then she walked home, picking up some okra and pumpkin from the market and stopping to buy a red cardboard bucket of chicken and chips from the Kentucky Fried Chicken as a treat for the kids.

'And my client would like nine other offences against Mother-care to be taken into consideration.'

Winsome was hardly paying attention. Although the judge had allowed her to remain seated throughout cross-examination because of the advanced stage of her pregnancy, the weight of her belly was making her back want to break.

Her eyes wandered over the green leather upholstery of the pale wooden benches. From the start of the case the courtroom had felt like an office, an office where everybody else had some reason for being there, some business to do, except her. People walked up to other people and whispered. This was a country full of whisperers. That was one of the odd things about England. Nothing was what it seemed. Everything was camouflaged – buildings especially. Courts masqueraded as offices; blocks of flats were built to resemble multi-storey car parks; their National Theatre pretended to be a prison and the new prisons were disguised as modern college buildings. People too. People concealed their intentions. And the people with power were not the extravagantly dressed ones, the people with power were the dowdy ones. Winsome wondered briefly if Sonia was giving the kids their tea. She had expected to be home by now. The judge, a nondescript man with glasses, was scribbling like a clerk in an invoice department. On the panelled wall over his head was a carved crest mounted on a board the shape of a shield. Woven in and out of crosses, lions and roses were some words that Winsome could not make out. They were written in funny lettering. The first word spelt HONI. Trying to decipher the rest gave her a headache. She had a strange sensation, as if a piece of string was connected from the back of her head to her left eye, pulling it out of focus. Then she heard the judge saying:

'I sentence you to twelve months' imprisonment.'

Everyone began to gather their papers together as if the day's work was over and it was time to go home. Winsome got up and vaguely prepared herself to go home too. A woman in a blue suit was plucking at her sleeve and saying in a kindly tone:

'Come along, dear.'

Sitting in the green prison van with its horizontally barred windows, Winsome was still unable to grasp what had happened. She somehow felt that the van would drop her off at home on the way to wherever it was going and she would be in time to give the kids their tea. The van threaded its way through the busy main streets of north London and stopped in front of some enormous gates in a high red brick wall. The gates opened and they went through. She and two other women got out. She found herself in an asphalt yard surrounded by more red brick walls. In one of the walls was a small door. Another screw in blue uniform was opening the door with one of the keys from the chain round her waist. She was beckoning to Winsome and beaming at her:

'It's all right, love,' she kept saying, 'this way, love.'

Dazed, Winsome followed her up some stone stairs to some double doors, the paint round the locks scuffed as if they had been repeatedly kicked. The word 'RECEPTION' was written on a sign overhead. In the cubicle where she had been told to undress she stood, hugely pregnant, trying to hold the coarse blue dressing-gown they had given her across her belly.

Then her waters broke all over the grey lino.

She lay in the hospital bed. Everything around seemed so white; the starched, white sheets on the bed; the nurses in their crisp white uniforms; the walls with their shiny white gloss paint. Winsome felt uncomfortably aware of her black face against the white pillows.

'You're seven centimetres dilated now. It won't be long,' said the ginger-haired nurse. Winsome turned her head away. The whiteness hurt her eyes. The pain was like a bad period pain, a long low ache in the back. Then the other pains started, rolling over her like a steam-roller. She was wheeled into the delivery room.

Back in the ward, Winsome slept. At her side, in his hospital cot, slept Denzil. Twelve hours after the birth, the prison authorities would come to take her and the child back to the prison. Some six hours after she had given birth, Winsome was awoken by the auxiliary cleaner bumping her mop against the legs of the bed. She looked up into the smiling, black, bespectacled face of the cleaner:

'Gal, you gat one beautiful pickney there. Is it a boy?'

Only half awake, Winsome nodded.

'Is wha' yuh gwaan call 'im?' The cleaner did not wait for Winsome to answer. She approached the head of the bed and said conspiratorially:

'No more kids for me, no sah! I done wid dat. Me periods dem stop, you know. An' lemme tell you, it is worse when dey stop dan when yuh gat dem. It was terrible. Terrible. Pain. Pain inna me belly all de time. An' the blood – it black. An' full of someting like cornmeal an' terrible bits.'

Winsome focused her eyes on the clock at the end of the ward. Seven fifteen a.m. In six hours they would come to take her back to prison. The cleaning woman took her mop and continued to talk:

'Black women strong, yuh know. Me mudda had me in de carner of a canefield and she was back at work a few hours later. I'm sixty-two. And another ting. Our blood is good and red. White women – dere blood is pale and weak and sarta watery. I seen it wid me own eyes in dis hospital.' She moved off down the ward with her mop and bucket.

Winsome looked over the side of the cot at the pale, brown baby, his flat puffy face crowned with a light black frizz. He was light-skinned now. He'll darken up later, she thought. More than anything she wanted to take him home, for the two of them to be reunited with Anita and Chantale. The sheet felt wet underneath her. Pulling back the bedclothes she saw a spreading scarlet stain. It was shaped like the poinciana tree in her grandmother's yard. She sat up and put her legs over the edge of the bed. Her body still felt big and bulky and misshapen and the stitches pulled inside her. She reached into the wooden locker next to her bed and felt for the hospital issue dressing-gown. She put it on. Nobody seemed to be taking any notice of her. She picked up Denzil and wrapped him carefully in the cot blanket, keeping a watchful eye on the nurses. Denzil felt limp and tiny and utterly relaxed. Winsome walked gingerly with him to the swing doors at the end of the ward and let herself through. The large corridor was empty. Uncertain how to operate the lift, Winsome began to descend the stairs holding the rail with her left hand, Denzil tucked into the crook of her right arm. One flight round the lift. A second flight and then she was opposite the main exit. A few more steps and she was outside the hospital.

Three-quarters of an hour later, Sonia looked down from her window into the yard of the flats when she heard the engine of a taxi ticking over. Alerted by a phone call, she had the money ready and ran down to pay off the cab. Winsome was climbing out of the cab awkwardly with the scrap of a baby in her arms.

Winsome rested exhaustedly in the low chair by the television, sipping a cup of tea. Her two daughters plucked and nuzzled and clambered over her and their new brother. Sonia stood at the stove frowning through her square-rimmed spectacles and pushing back the shoulder-length beaded extensions on her hair. The action of the judge in jailing Winsome more or less the day the baby was expected had so enraged Sonia that she dismissed the consequences of helping her. She looked through the doorway at the heavy, defeated shape of the woman in the chair:

'What are we gonna do?' asked Sonia. Winsome shrugged. Denzil yawned and she automatically loosened the blanket round him so that he could stretch his legs and kick a little. Then she dozed again. From the kitchen window Sonia saw the police car arrive in the yard. Her heart beat faster. The car remained in the yard, its blue light spinning, while two policemen ran up the five flights of stairs to where Winsome lived. It was the flat above Sonia's. Sonia heard the sound of the door being forced and then the sound of footsteps wandering about over her head. She watched as they left. Winsome slept. Sonia tried to telephone Junior but there was no reply.

At one o'clock the two women watched with fascination as a picture of Winsome appeared on the mid-day news programme. A suitably grave and concerned newscaster made the following announcement:

'The Home Office is concerned over the welfare of a twenty-five-year-old woman prisoner who escaped from a hospital in north London early today only hours after giving birth to a baby son. The Home Office fears that the woman may be suffering from post-natal depression and the baby is said to have infantile hypothermia. The Home Office want the woman and child to be returned to custody as soon as possible so that they can be properly cared for and given the attention they require.'

Winsome was sitting upright:

'What did they say was wrong with the baby?' she asked Sonia. She unwrapped the child and examined him carefully. He slept contentedly. 'I can't see anything wrong with him.' The words had sounded ominous, like those other mumbo-jumbo words Levi had warned her about in the courtroom.

'That's just a trap to get you back into jail,' said Sonia shrewdly. Winsome hugged her baby and at the same time managed to wipe down Chantale's face with the corner of a handkerchief:

'I'll have to go back in the end, I suppose,' she said, recognising the inevitable. Sonia wanted to make her outrage known, to make some sort of protest. It was Sonia who began to cry. She sat on the brown leather pouffe wiping the tears from the corner of her eyes:

'You know,' she said, 'I don't go in for all this Rasta business but sometimes what Levi says is true. They are wicked, evil people these Babylon people. If you've got to go back there then we should make one gigantic fuss about it. You must get 'pon de television and mek dem see what these people dem a do to you. Mek dem see you side of the story.' In her excitement, Sonia slipped back and forth from cockney to patois.

'Does Junior know about the baby?' asked Winsome suddenly.

'Junior don't even know you got a sentence yet. Everything happen so quick. I phone him but he ain' there. What do you think – shall I ring up the television people or do you want to try and stay out?'

'I won't be able to stay out long, not with the baby, so you can do what you like. Just let me stay here the night and I'll go back tomorrow.'

Winsome was enjoying being in a place of colour after the arid courtroom, the drained grey jail and the pristine hospital. Sonia had a brightly patterned red and black carpet. A May breeze was catching and blowing the net curtains and the colour television in the corner of the room was like a burst of flowers. Sonia's little boy Marlon came to look at the new baby:

'He's a nice boy, innit Marlon?' said Winsome. Marlon nodded.

'OK,' said Sonia. 'I'll go to the shops. Don't answer the door.'

During the afternoon, Winsome occasionally peeked out of the window. People came and went in the streets, in and out of the banks, the greengrocers and the hardware stores. Everything appeared to be a mockery of normality. The people looked like extras in a film, acting out everyday life for the cameras.

Sonia shopped, burning all the while with rage.

Winsome gave Denzil his first bath and oiled his little brown body, pleased to administer these rites in an ordinary bathroom, hung with lines of little shorts and T-shirts. At tea-time, she automatically fed the two little girls and Marlon.

'Can you take care of the girls for me, Sonia?' she asked when eventually Sonia returned, laden with plastic carrier bags. 'I don't want my mum to get her hands on them. She don't treat them right. But she'll always help you out with money and so will Junior.'

'Course I will. Me tek good care o' dem an' me bring dem up to see you. And as soon as I find Junior I tell him to come straight down to see you and the baby. Listen Winsome, you're not just going back like that. It's disgusting what they do to you. Mek we phone those television people so you go back with everybody knowing just what is going on.'

'I don't feel no way about it. Do what you want,' said Winsome. 'Phone them in the morning. I'm going to bed for a bit.'

The television crew had difficulty setting up the lights and cameras in Sonia's small front room with the kids running about and playing. The television journalist who smelt of after-shave lotion asked Winsome to move her chair a little bit further from the window. Winsome noticed how the bright artificial lights drained the room of colour and made everything harsh and pale. She still had a headache. She moved her chair, clutching Denzil in one arm. The production assistant fumbled with her clip-board and tried to prevent Anita and Marlon having a tug-of-war with an electric cable.

'Now then.' The newsman was embarrassed now that he was face to face with the silent black woman with the scar on her lip. 'What I thought was I'd ask you one or two questions and, maybe, ask your friend here what she thinks and then, if you're going to give yourself up anyway, which you say you are, we could give you a lift back to the prison and take a final shot of you walking into the jail with the baby to sort of finish the story off. If that's OK with you. I don't want to put any pressure on you. So is that OK?'

Winsome nodded. Sonia perched anxiously on the edge of an armchair, puffing at a cigarette. The camera started to roll, taking in pictures of Winsome sitting in the low chair with Denzil in her arms and Chantale sucking her thumb and holding on to her mother's skirt. In hushed and sympathetic tones the newsman asked:

'Why did you run away from the hospital?'

The lights were white and hot. Winsome became aware of two cold patches of sweat under her arms. She did not know what was required, what to say:

'I don't know,' she replied, barely audible. Her hand comforted Chantale at her skirt. The camera swung from Winsome's expressionless face to Sonia. Sonia looked bright and defiant. She had dressed specially for the interview in her new, red nylon blouse and her gold chains:

'I think it's terrible that a judge should send someone to jail for a year just when she's due to have a baby. I think it was a wicked thing to do.' Sonia sounded clear and cool. Winsome just wanted it all to stop.

'Thanks, that's fine,' said the newsman. 'Let's pack up now and take all the stuff down to the prison and then we can get that last shot – if that's OK with you, Winsome.'

Winsome rose awkwardly from the chair and began to collect a few bits and pieces for herself and the baby. Sonia was to stay behind with the other children.

'God, I feel awful,' giggled the production assistant behind her clip-board to the director. 'I feel as if I'd captured a runaway slave or something.'

The cameras trained on Winsome as she walked with the baby up to the main entrance of the modern jail building. She entered the door where the gate-man sat behind bullet-proof glass operating the electronic sliding doors. He grinned:

'Hello, love. Come back to us, have you? I'll ring up to the mother and baby unit and get someone to come down and fetch you.'

Winsome sat silent on the bench just inside the entrance.

Two minutes later a blue-uniformed screw appeared to collect her. She had badly permed blonde hair and the face of a retarded schoolgirl. She spoke with a northern accent:

'Hello Winifred. Oh we are pleased to see you back safe and sound. You were a naughty girl to run off like that. We were all worried to death. Let me have a look at the baby. Ahhhhhh. Isn't he gorgeous.'

The news item appeared on the early evening news. By the late evening news it had already been replaced by bigger and more important stories.

That night, Winsome slept, worn out, with Denzil by her side, in a cell as cheerless as a public lavatory which someone had made a feeble attempt to decorate with one or two pictures.

The dream came back, but this time a little altered. She dreamt that she was in unfamiliar countryside. The execution must have taken place for she was already dead and being carried in a funeral procession. But she was not in a coffin. The hands of strangers were bearing her body along. Close to, the terrain was rocky and the path narrow, wending its way through bare, hilly landscape. The bearers moved carefully to avoid the big clumps of wild grass. All she could see ahead was the long, empty, winding path. Resting on her chest were some bright flowers. They seemed familiar. She tried hard to remember the names of them. But the names wouldn't come.

Everybody knows that Tuxedo has good ideas about as often as a hen has teeth. Which is why Tuxedo is on his own this particular night, crouching with his ear to the tumbrils of a small safe behind the counter of the video shop. The snag is that Tuxedo is not built for crouching lower than a pool table. His left foot has cramp and his blue satin boxer shorts are twisted in his crotch causing him aggravation. On top of all this, twiddling the knobs on the safe is getting him nowhere and he is overcome by a craving for sweet potato pie.

Anybody, from the Frontline to the Backline, could tell you that Tuxedo is jinxed. Take one instance. Yesterday Tuxedo buys a second-hand car for three hundred and fifty, cash. This guy gives him all the documents but when he gets home the log book turns out to be an old parking summons and the car is clearly hotter than Tina Turner; if Tuxedo thinks he has just laid his hands on some pure Jamaican sensimilla, you can bet your bottom dollar that it will turn out to be home-grown from Kensal Rise; even the all-night Kentucky Fried Chicken runs out of corn on the cob as soon as Tuxedo steps through the portals. Anybody could tell you that the day Tuxedo gets lucky will be the day it snows ink. Which is why he has this near-permanent frowning glare on his face, a wicked screw that most people mistake for hostility when in fact it's the anxious stare of one who knows that God has been up most of the night laying traps for him, sometimes in the shape of things, mostly in the shape of people.

Tuxedo glares at the safe:

'Come on, you bastard,' he mutters, then adds: 'It's all right, God, it's the safe I'm talking to, not you.'

Of one thing, Tuxedo is certain. God is white. Once, when he was younger, he had listened to his militant cousin explain how white people had tricked the world into believing that Jesus was white when he was really black and so it followed that God was black too, or at least brown, more likely brown seeing that he was from the Middle East. Tuxedo told all this to his mother who gave him several licks for daring to call God 'a dutty half-breed'. In the end, Tuxedo came to his own conclusion, simple and to the point. If God isn't white, how come black people have such a hard time?

Anyway, Tuxedo is in this office which is short of space what with the desk and the metal filing cabinets. The light is on because Tuxedo doesn't much like the dark ever since the school caretaker accidentally locked him in the boiler room where he was hiding because he couldn't remember the lyrics of the seven-times table. Since then, Tuxedo gets jittery in the dark. So he is tackling his first safe, solo, with the light on in the back of Edwards Electronic and TV Rental shop. As it happens, he has only discovered the safe by chance, stubbing his toe against it while he is in the back of the shop looking for some Vaseline.

The reason Tuxedo is looking for Vaseline is this. He has broken into the shop to get a video recorder for Dolores Burton, his current mainsqueeze. Now all the episodes of *Hill Street Blues* would lead you to believe that during the commission of these minor felonies, people break out in a nervous sweat. Just when the music gets tense and trembly and the camera goes into close-up, you can see sweat streaming down their faces. Not so Tuxedo. His face goes all dry and cracky, especially the lips, which prompts him to put down the video recorder and look in the back of the shop on the offchance of finding some Vaseline or even a little Johnson's baby oil to rub in his face. And this is precisely what he is doing when the safe attracts the attention of his big toe.

Outside, the August night is warm. The street is still strewn with litter from the market and the sweet glutinous smell of rotting vegetables hangs in the air. The street lamps cast a bilious glow over the row of shops. Parked outside the video shop is Tuxedo's getaway car, a powder-blue Vauxhall Chevette, the same one he got yesterday. The choice of this particular model, he considers to be a stroke of genius. Any passing beast would think it belonged to an estate agent or a lady doctor. Not that many lady doctors park their cars outside a video shop at three in the morning with the driver's door open and the sound cassette pumping out into the night air:

> 'Trouble you de trouble mi – no I
> I woudda jus' flash me ting.'

The car chants away rhythmically to itself. A few doors down, the burglar alarm in the chemist's shop shrills montonous and unattended. Tuxedo twists the knobs on the safe impatiently. Nobody is about.

Nobody is about that is except Frankie Formosa, known to his girlfriends as 'Mr Too Handsome to Work' who happens to stroll around the corner on his way back from picking up a ten pound draw from Mr Mighty's Ace Shebeen. He is draining the last drop from a can of vanilla nutriment so he doesn't at first spot the car. But just as he throws the empty can into the gutter, he sights up the means of transport that would save him a fifteen-minute walk back to Ladbroke Grove. Besides, there is no one around to admire him walking through the streets in his new Tachini tracksuit and trainers to match. Don't think that Frankie is in any way unfit enough for such a walk. Frankie is always super-plus fit when he comes out of jail because he spends all his time there in the gym. Although this time he could not get all the exercise he wanted on account of a little squirt called Mouth-Mouth. Mouth-Mouth is Frankie's sister's boyfriend and it is sheer bad luck that he turns up in jail at the same time as Frankie because Frankie did not really want it known that he was inside for such a minor offence as driving round the streets without a licence and had put it about that he was in jail for the more prestigious and universally popular offence of assaulting a policeman. Then Mouth-Mouth comes in and spills the beans which meant that it was Mouth-Mouth who got assaulted and

Frankie had to continue getting what excercise he could in the restricting confines of the punishment block.

So Frankie pulls to a halt on the opposite side of the road to the Chevette.

'Yuh free to look but don' you dare stare,' chants the car happily. But Frankie is not staring. He is giving quick looks up and down the street checking out whether Fate has actually come up trumps and offered him a deserted street and an unlocked car at one and the same time. He crosses back towards the car. On the pavement are large fragments of glass from the plate glass door. The door itself swings carelessly on its hinges and although there is a light on in the back, nobody seems to be there. This is because Tuxedo is bent double on the floor having about as much luck with the combination on the safe as he did with his seven times table. Frankie waits for a moment or two in the doorway of the Ace Liquor Mart.

> 'When something good – we say it Bad.
> Bubble you de bubble mi – yes I
> I woudda jus' dip an' run een.'

The car has now given up all pretensions of good breeding and is singing in a gruff, suggestive voice to the accompanying sounds of a deep thumping bass and whistling bullets. Frankie peeps out warily from the doorway. Nobody in sight. He slips round the front of the car and slides into the driver's seat, shutting the door gently behind him. Ten seconds later, Frankie Formosa is heading smoothly towards the block of flats in Notting Hill Gate which the council uses to house, temporarily, people they don't like.

Tuxedo has cramp. He shifts and stands up. He abandons the attempt to open the safe in the shop and decides to take it home with him along with the video cassette recorder. That will impress Dolores. On the desk is a grubby cream telephone and Tuxedo is sorely tempted to give Dolores a bell just to show how cool his nerve is under pressure. Sensing, however, that time like most things is not on his side, he resists the impulse. Which is just as well because Dolores has long time since taken her tail off to Ozo's Club where she is sandwiched between two gentlemen both with wet-look hairstyles smothered in Dax pomade and each competing with the other as to who can buy her one of the over-priced drinks at the bar.

Life never deals out a hand of entirely bum cards. Mr George Evans, proprietor and manager of Edwards Electronics is a man for whom the notion of good salesmanship is twinned with the notion of well-greased hair. In the third drawer of the desk, Tuxedo comes across Mr Evans' king-size jar of Vaseline pure petroleum jelly. And it is while he is rubbing it on his face that he becomes aware of a change of sounds from outside. The raunchy upful beat from his car has been replaced by the disjointed, mechanical, crackling voices that spurt so unexpectedly from the radios policemen wear on their chests. Tuxedo steps cautiously from the lighted office holding up the jar of Vaseline like a candle. In the darkened exterior of the shop he makes out three silhouettes, one of them pushing away broken glass with its foot.

Wappen Bappen – Tuxedo is under arrest.

It takes him five seconds to decide against pleading racial harassment and on his face as he walks sheepishly to the door is the same expression of disgust, disbelief and exasperation as when he misses an easy shot in the snooker hall. This expression changes when he reaches the street. His delicate pale blue ladies' saloon car has metamorphosed into a big, business-like Rover with jazzy red and blue markings and a revolving blue light on top, for all the world like it is the Metropolitan Police mobile disco.

'Just a minute. Just a minute,' says Tuxedo in pure bewilderment before accepting the invitation from two of the police to step in the back of the car. The third one remains behind reasoning seriously with his radio.

The night sky has that purplish haze and Tuxedo catches sight of it between the faded, peeling, white house fronts. He is gazing up in that direction because he is conducting one of his silent conversations with the Almighty as the car cruises along:

'You bastard. Yes guy, it's you I'm talkin' to. Nuff trouble you

give me. Spiteful I call it. Fucking spite.' Tuxedo talks to God in
the same way he talks to the police, in his London accent, saving
the Jamaican for his mates. Then suddenly he remembers the
small packet of herb in his underpants. Casually, he slips his
hand into the elasticated waistband of his boxer shorts. The
move goes unnoticed. He slips his hand further down and starts
fishing imperceptibly for the tiny packet of ganga secreted in his
yellow underpants. All the while, he stares morosely out of the
car window. One discrete cough and Tuxedo has in his mouth
about two square inches of 'The Voice' newspaper, umpteen
seeds and bits of stick as well as several heads and leaves of
ganga.

'Lock the fucker in the cell if he won't talk.' Detective Sergeant
Blake sounds weary. Tuxedo's mother has taught him never to
speak with his mouth full. 'Check with the owner what's missing
from the shop.' Tuxedo is taken downstairs and put in the fourth
cell along the row.

One hour later, Mr Evans of Edwards Electronics has
checked and double-checked and confirmed to the remaining
policeman that the only item missing from the premises is the
pot of Vaseline. Tuxedo is sprawling on a hard bed with the grey
blanket wrapped round him and one big smile on his face. He
has discovered that he can talk to God Jamaica-style like one
black man to another. It makes God feel more like one of the
boys:

'Is wha' mi a go do? Oonoo help mi nuh? Is jus' one lickle
degi-degi ting me a tek, one lickle pot of cream fi oil mi face. Mi
a hear seh yuh work in mysterious ways. Show mi nuh. Don'
gwaan bad about it. Remember Tuxedo don' business wid
voilence.'

The more Tuxedo chats in this confidential manner, the more
he realises that things are not nearly as bad as they might be. He
could have been caught with the stolen Chevette, the video
machine, the office safe and a bunch of weed. As it is, there is
only the Vaseline to be reckoned with. A little fine probably.
Dolores will no doubt kick up because her favourite tape has
gone with the car. Tuxedo thinks of Dolores for a minute, tucked
up under the candlewick bedspread, her right hand under her
jaw, which is how she sleeps, and wonders if there is any sweet

potato pie left in the fridge. Tuxedo wants to get back to Dolores and hug her up for a while. He gets this rush of warmth towards her which spills over and includes God. On the whole, events have not turned out too badly:

'Yes mi baas,' says Tuxedo to God. 'Now me see how it is yuh work dis ting out fi me in the best possible way.'

In the charge room, Detective Sergeant Blake is getting confused as he tries to take down Tuxedo's statement:

'So you broke into the TV shop . . .'

'To get some Vaseline,' adds Tuxedo, helpfully.

'Why didn't you go into the chemist's?'

'The chemist's was shut,' says Tuxedo.

Detective Sergeant Blake decides to charge Tuxedo quickly and go home. Tuxedo has much the same idea. Once charged, he asks if it is OK for him to go now and get ready to appear in court in the morning in case the magistrates do not fully appreciate the vision of him appearing before them in his boxer shorts.

'You're not going anywhere,' says Blake tetchily. 'We haven't been able to establish that the address you gave is the correct one. So you will stay here and we will take you to court in the morning.'

'Phone my girlfriend. She's at home,' protests Tuxedo.

'We've already tried phoning twice and a constable has called round there. There's nobody there.'

Mystified, Tuxedo allows himself to be led back to cell number four.

'What's the time?' he asks anxiously, as the policeman is about to bang the door to.

'Half past four.'

Where is Dolores? Why isn't she asleep in bed the one night he needs her to be in? Where the hell is Dolores?

Tuxedo is mightily vex. He walks up and down the cell for a bit then looks at the window which is set high up in the wall. The top is curved, the bars are painted cream, the panes are of unbreakable, dingy plastic. Behind them the sun is beginning to rise. He crosses the room and stands on tip-toe to look out.

'White bastard!' he yells at the pale, dawn sky.

On that particular Tuesday afternoon in July, it rained. Then it stopped. Then it rained again, making the streets wet, steamy and hot. The herbalist shop in one of the shabbier districts of south London was packed with customers. One stout, black, elderly woman in spectacles and a blue felt hat was leaning across the counter whispering in the assistant's ear:

'I want sometin' for me husband. 'E caan stop goin'. 'E runnin' to the toilet all the while.' The pale assistant with the pale-rimmed glasses looked as though vegetable juice ran in her veins. She answered benignly:

'We have Cranesbill for urinary incontinence.'

'What?' The old woman screwed up her face.

'Cranesbill for urinary incontinence,' the assistant said a little louder.

'What's that? I don' hear so good.'

'Cranesbill for a weak bladder,' shouted the assistant, causing a titter in the crowd.

'Yes. Gimme some o' dat. An' some tincture of cloves for me tooth.'

The assistant made up the order briskly and neatly. Behind her on the wall hung one of the original, old-fashioned advertisements for 'Balsam of Lungwort containing Horehound and Aniseed – A Boon to the Afflicted'. The shop had been there since the beginning of the century. In the fifties it nearly closed through lack of trade. Then the black people started to arrive. Business picked up. As word spread, African and Caribbean people from all over London came seeking poke root for sore throats; senna pods for their bowels; fever grass for their colds;

green camphor ointment; slippery elm; Irish moss; Jamaican sorrel; eucalyptus leaves; until Mr Goodwin, the latest in a long line of Goodwins, far from shutting up shop, was obliged to take on two more assistants and one extra person to serve at the Sarsparilla counter.

Now, Mr Goodwin stood patiently dispensing the order of two French hippies, the only white customers, who were taking an inordinately long time browsing through the list of potions and powders and gums and roots and barks, sniffing at herbs and examining tinctures of asafoetida and red capsicum with little crooning noises of surprise and delight. They were unaware of the jostling throng of some twenty people behind them. Wedged amongst these was a small, black boy of about ten, gazing about him in astonishment. He had thickly protruding lips and his head was closely shaven. In each ear sat a grey, plastic hearing-aid the shape of Africa. The man at his side was restless and edgy. Jittery. His forehead kept wrinkling into a frown. His frizzy hair had something unkempt about it. His teeth were small and jagged. He wore a sweater, grey with a green diamond pattern on it, frayed at the neck and his trousers were old, brown and shapeless. Round his neck hung two silver chains, one carrying a small, gold box and the other a miniature pistol, which is why he was known as Pistol-Man. He looked vexed and was making small noises of dissatisfaction. When a young black woman pushed in front of him he could contain himself no longer:

'Hey! You pushin' in front of me. I don' come all the way from north London to wait at the back of the line. She pushin' in front of me,' he complained. Then he rounded indignantly on two other people he had seen edging their way towards the front. 'An' I see you pushin' in front of them.' He started to wave his arms like the conductor of a large orchestra. 'An' them people,' he indicated a mother and child at the back, 'was here before you,' he tapped on the shoulder of a pompous-looking Trinidadian with a moustache. The man shrugged him off:

'Cool it, nuh. Cool it nuh, man. Everythin' cool till yuh open yuh big mouth. There ain' no lines.'

The man with the pistol round his neck looked fit to explode:

'That's what I say. There ain' no lines.' He threw up his hands in distress as if the disorder in the shop was somehow representative of all the disorder in the world; the chaos in Beirut; the turmoil in Sri-Lanka; the upheavals in the Philippines and to some extent the confusion in himself, and if only he could organise it properly, that and everything else in the world would be set to rights. Then, out of the corner of his eye, he spotted a gap in the crowd ahead of him and stepped quickly into it.

'Now you pushin' in front of me.' The tall, light-skinned woman with the red head-wrap smiled as she accused Pistol-Man. He looked abashed, mortified:

'I know,' he said, looking round the room defensively, 'but I was goin' to let you go before me. I'm fair.' He spoke loud enough for everyone to hear. On the other side of the shop he saw someone he recognised:

'Hello! Hello, Mrs Ebanks. You still livin' in Stoke Newington? Long time I don' see you.'

'Yes, we still there.' The middle-aged woman stood stolidly beside her husband as if they were waiting for the millennium. Dismay crossed Pistol-Man's face as he watched someone push in front of them:

'You shouldn't let people push in front of you. You been waitin' long?'

'We fine, tank you.' They stood stock still, both with their hands folded in front of them as though they were about to burst into hymns. Pistol-Man couldn't stop himself talking:

'Look,' he said to nobody in particular, 'I'm nearly there. Why it takin' so long? Some people have to get back to work. People got things to do,' he said, righteously, although he himself fell into neither category. The main reason it was taking so long was because the French couple, oblivious to all that was going on behind them, were taking their time, fingering bottles with squeaks of pleasure and ordering remedy after remedy. Pistol-Man continued his beef:

'I got to get two buses to reach home and it nearly rush hour.'

'You mekin' fuss,' boomed the surly Trinidadian with the moustache. Pistol-Man continued to grumble:

'Everybody look at you as if you mad but if I din' make fuss I never reach where I am now.' He looked round for approval and smiled with relief when a wave of laughter swept through the assembled customers. An African girl turned round to him and said in her clipped accent:

'What you are saying is true. I know it is true because look how I push in front of you.' She had a big smile and gold ear-rings.

'Yes,' he replied, 'but you laughin' so that's all right.' Secretly, Pistol-Man was a bit wary of Africans. He believed that while the West Indians, like himself, came to the shop in search of cures, the Africans probably came to buy herbs that would make people ill.

Finally, triumphantly, he reached the counter. Then he remembered the cinnamon-skinned woman in the red head-wrap:

'Do you still want to come in front of me?' he asked, politely. Vera Mullins did indeed want to be served first. She had been on duty at the hospital since six in the morning and her feet were aching.

'Yes,' she said, moving forward to address the woman behind the counter. 'It's for my friend,' she explained. 'Her glands are all swollen in her neck and under her arms.'

'We can't really treat that,' said the assistant. 'That is likely to be a sympton of something else and we would need to know . . .'

'Lavender oil,' interrupted Pistol-Man loudly from behind Vera's shoulder. 'Give she lavender oil.'

Vera Mullins began to laugh. But she bought some lavender oil anyway. As she waited for it to be wrapped, the clean smell of peppermint floated into her nostrils from somewhere, reminding her of her grandmother in St Vincent whose clothes always smelt of peppermint and bay rum. People in the shop were now laughing and talking noisily. That too reminded her of home and the market in Kingstown. Taking herself completely by surprise she found herself turning round to address the shoppers:

'All right,' she said. 'I driving back to Finsbury Park. Is who needs a lift in that direction – north London?' Pistol-Man was busy at the counter ordering the bitter aloes that settled his stomach after too many cans of McEwans Export Strong Lager. He cocked his ear, unable to believe his luck:

'I do,' he said quickly.

'What about those other people from Stoke Newington?'

Vera pointed towards Mr and Mrs Ebanks, who were standing, rooted to the same spot, having made no progress.

'The lady says do you want a lift home?' called Pistol-Man, in his cracked voice, gesticulating over the heads of waiting customers.

'No tanks,' replied Mrs Ebanks. 'We fine. We jus' wait and take our time till it get less busy.'

'Anyone else?' asked Vera, turning her head from side to side, expectantly. Brown, almond-shaped eyes looked enquiringly from a passive, oval face. Pistol-Man was staring at Vera with a mixture of pleasure and suspicious curiosity. He fingered the day's growth of stubble on his chin and wished he had shaved that morning. Alarmed to find that Pistol-Man was the only volunteer, Vera, for an instant, regretted her offer. She could feel something fractious and nervy about the man. London was full of dangerous strangers, unlike St Vincent. No one else took up the offer. She managed a smile:

'My car's round the corner,' she said.

Outside, rain speckled the pavement like a bird's egg. They walked past the drab shops, Pistol-Man talking fast and furious as a fire-cracker to disguise his self-consciousness. Somehow, the more he prattled, the more calm Vera Mullins became.

'Yes,' he said. 'Lavender oil is good, you know. Very good.' His accent was cockney, grafted on to some now indistinguishable Caribbean base. 'It helped get the swelling down when my tooth was bad. I was in terrible pain that time. Two dentists I went to and they couldn't see nothing wrong and then the third one found this tiny, tiny hole that was givin' all the trouble. He said it was the minutest hole he had ever come across,' boasted Pistol-Man, pleased to have suffered from a condition that defied medical expertise. It made him feel different. Unique. It was for that same reason that when the council allocated him a basement flat in a house converted into Flats 1, 2 and 3, he had taken down the notice that said Flat 1, and written FLAT A on a piece of card and stuck it on the front door. It made him feel different. It was a matter of distinction.

As they rounded the corner, Vera realised that the little black boy with the deaf-aids was scurrying along behind them. Pistol-Man turned to see where she was looking:

'Oh yeah,' said Pistol-Man. 'That's my son. He's deaf and dumb from he was born. I raise him.'

It was Vera's turn to feel curious. As she unlocked the door of the old, blue Ford with rusted streaks along its side, she caught the boy looking at her. His eyes were eager, full of merriment and intelligence, as if he were about to say something of great importance. If you could speak, she found herself thinking, you would say something beautiful. Suddenly, she felt safer about giving a lift to this talkative stranger who crackled with tension. Safer now that she knew the child would be with them:

'What's his name?' she asked.

'Avalon,' replied Pistol-Man. 'I named him that. I found it in a book of myths. I think it's Greek,' he added.

Avalon. Avalon. Where wounded heroes go to rest. Where King Arthur went to heal his wounds. The boy scrambled into the back of the car.

'Sorry. This car is a tip,' Vera apologised. Pistol-Man raised his head to the heavens and cackled incredulously. The woman saved him the fares, saved him a long tedious wait in bus queues. As if he would care about a little mess. He would have been grateful for a ride in a donkey cart. They set off through the wet street, full of litter from the market. Pistol-Man crowed with delight inside himself for having secured a ride, as if he had outwitted the Fates for once. But he talked non-stop, through a sort of shyness. He couldn't make the woman out. Because she said so little, he talked all the more. Because he did not often have the chance to talk, everything about his life and his son came out in a torrent:

'He's got five per cent hearing. He's all right. He can lip-read. He can do sign language. And he can lie as good as any normal boy,' added the father proudly. 'He's so convincing, you wouldn't believe it.' Vera glanced over her shoulder at the child who could weave falsehoods with his hands. Avalon was sitting with his head twisted round trying to look at an old magazine on the floor of the car.

'Sometimes he's sad,' continued Pistol-Man, 'because no friends come to see us. I tell him friends will come some day. I quarrelled with my family, you see. I don't see them no more. It's just me and him now. It's a good thing to have a close family.' He said it with regret, as if a family was something that had somehow passed him by, out of reach. The truth was that Pistol-Man quarrelled with everybody. He was a quarrelsome man, pig-headed, easily annoyed, impatient, fretful.

'He's at a Special School now. He's going to boarding school in September. Then I can get back to my music. I'm a musician you see. I want to form my own band. I've worked with other bands and it's no good. The people they make excuses. They don't turn up. There's too much hassle. Too much pressure. An' then I get vex, you see and I blow my top because the people them drive me mad. I can see it's goin' to happen but I can't stop it. I wish I could be six people at once, then I could be all the members of the band.'

'Dad-dee.' The hard-to-form words came from the back of the car. Pistol-Man turned to the boy. In the driving-mirror, Vera could see the boy's hands moving like butterflies. His father signed a reply.

'You can talk sign language?' asked Vera.

'I'm not very good at it, though,' said Pistol-Man modestly. 'I just told him "Lady give lift home".'

As they edged through the rush-hour traffic, rain spotting the windscreen, Pistol-Man threw a sly, sidelong look at the woman sitting impassively at the wheel beside him:

'You could be giving a lift to a mad person,' he said. 'A killer person.'

'I trusted you because of the child.' As she spoke, Vera remembered she had offered the lift before knowing the child was with him. Pistol-Man had his face pressed to the window. She turned and smiled at Avalon who grinned with pleasure in return.

'He's all right.' Pistol-Man looked over his shoulder at the boy. 'He knows that whatever I have, he has too. We share everything. We're equal.' His head jerked round as something in the street caught his attention. 'D'you see that shop? They sell fluffy things in there that you can sit on and they roll out into sleeping bags. They're fluffy.' He said it with relish. 'I can't afford one. They're about eighty pounds.' The quietness of the woman seeped into him, soothing him. Out of the blue, he said:

'Some people calm people down. They could get attacked but it goes the other way.' He wished he had not been so loudmouthed in the herbalist's. 'You mek fuss and people look at you as if you were mad, but if you don't mek fuss people walk all over you,' he muttered, half to himself.

'Which road do you want?' asked Vera.

'Amhurst Road. Round to the left here. Do you know Hackney?'

'Yes.'

'Did you know that this bit is Amhurst Road too?' He made it sound as though it was his special secret.

'Yes.'

'Most people don't know that,' he said with approval. 'Most people think it ends further up. Here we are. Pull up by that tree.' The man and the boy got out of the car:

'Bye . . . Bye.' Avalon made the sounds a diver makes speaking under water.

'Just a minute. Just a minute. Would you like to come in for a drink?' Pistol-Man's forehead wrinkled into worried lines as he peered through the car window at her. She felt drawn to the man and the child. It can't do any harm, she thought.

To Pistol-Man's exasperation, the key stuck in the lock of the basement door. Avalon pulled a face at Vera that said clearly 'Oh no, not again!' Finally the key turned and they stepped into a small, dark passage and then into the back room.

'Sit down. Sit down.' He waved his guest towards an old settee with a crumpled, stone-coloured duvet on it that he pulled over himself at nights as he lay watching television.

'Wait there a minute,' he said. 'I've got to get him his tea.' He felt awkward, unused to visitors. He disappeared into the kitchen, shutting the door behind him so that she would not see the washing-up piled in the sink. Vera looked round the room. The walls were painted yellow ochre. The furniture was cheap and ugly. On the floor was a grey carpet as thin as cardboard. On the mantel-piece rested a semi-circular mirror flanked on either side by two big, plastic Coca Cola bottles. Pistol-Man had cut the tops of these to use them as jars which held an assortment of rulers and pencils. Opposite her, under the low dresser, was a jumble of plimsolls and trainers belonging to the man and the boy. Piles of papers and folders were stashed untidily about the place. From the kitchen came the sound of something frizzling in the pan.

Avalon stood in the centre of the room with an expression of intense concentration on his face. Then he raised one hand, the finger pointed, as if to say, 'I know what to do'. He dived for his black school bag and showed Vera his pencil-case and some of his school books. He puzzled for a moment over what else he could do to entertain the guest. Then he ran to the sideboard and showed her the school photograph of himself smiling, framed in white card. He scratched his head, then remembered the snakes. Two yellow traffic lanterns that Pistol-Man had stolen from the street adorned the dresser. Looped around the handle of each was a wooden, jointed snake, one brightly painted in pink, the other in green. Avalon pointed to the pink one and pointed to himself. Then he pointed to the green one and said laboriously:

'My . . . dad.'

Vera found the boy delightful. She pointed to a painting on a piece of paper, sellotaped to the wall. It was a picture of a boot with 'The Rogue Brogue' written underneath it with an exclamation mark.

'Did you do that?' she asked. He shook his head.

'My . . . dad,' he said again.

Pistol-Man elbowed his way into the room carrying a plate with two hamburgers on it and some spaghetti from a tin. He put the food on the formica-topped table and turned to Avalon. He spoke and used sign language at the same time:

'Go and put your pyjamas on.' He explained to Vera, 'I have to tell him to do that because he gets his clothes dirty and it's me has to wash them. Do you want a drink? I've got McEwans Lager because that's what I drink.'

'I don't drink alcohol. Have you got any juice?' She hoped this would not prove awkward for him but for a minute Pistol-Man looked flummoxed:

'Ribena,' he said, 'I've got some Ribena.' He returned from the kitchen with a tumbler so brimful of the red liquid that he nearly spilled it.

'I hope that's not too sweet. Is it too sweet?' he enquired anxiously.

'It's fine,' she said. Avalon bounced back into the room wearing a pair of white cotton pyjamas with navy-blue triangles on them. His presence relieved the sexual tension between the man and the woman. Pistol-Man straddled a chair by the table as Avalon sat down to eat his meal. He pulled the metal ring off his can of lager:

'Yeah. This is where I always am, every evening, with my cans of beer. I have to stay in, you see, because of him. He can't ever say to me "You have more fun than me because you're grown-up", because he sees that I stay in too. We both stay in. He knows that everything I have, I share with him. We're both the same. Both equal. Sometimes, he pretends to be worse than he is. Pistol-Man put his hand to his ear and pulled a sad face, mimicking the boy. "I'm deaf," he says, "I'm deaf." And I say, "Yes, I know you're bloody deaf." And we both laugh.' He took a gulp of lager. 'It's a sacrifice I make, you see. No. Not a sacrifice.' He hunted for the right word. 'No. It's a dedication.' He looked over at the boy. 'I growed him and I raised him. It's like putting money in the bank. An investment. You watch it grow. Only it's love. I'm not really a materialist. I'm more a spiritual sort of man.'

More or less the only trips Pistol-Man ever made were to the betting-shop round the corner which he visited as often as possible, optimism springing afresh in his breast on every occasion. He pulled his chair round to face the woman squarely.

'Now, I'm going to interrogate you,' he said. 'What do you do?'

'I'm a nurse,' said Vera.

'Where do you come from?'

'St Vincent – a long time ago.'

'I'm from Buxton in Guyana,' he said. 'I don't remember that much either.' He scrutinised his new friend. She sipped her Ribena. Usually, he would have said to a woman like that 'You're looking nice and slim' or 'That's a nice outfit you're wearing,' but something about this woman prevented him from doing so. He took in her honey-coloured skin and slanting, serious, brown eyes. His own skin was dark.

'There's some Portuguese in my family somewhere,' he said. 'Portuguese are white people, you know.' He rolled up the sleeve of his sweater and inspected his forearm as if expecting to see white patches appear magically on the brown.

'I like you,' he said, looking directly at her. 'Yes. I like you.'

Vera thought that she should leave soon. Avalon was busy on

the floor, drawing something with a ruler and pencil. Suddenly, Pistol-Man spotted the dirty plate on the table and leapt to his feet. Vera almost laughed at the tableau they made: the man pointing sternly at the plate and the boy with his eyes widening in dismay, his hand over his mouth. The boy's deafness had made both of them expressive in face and gesture, like actors in a silent movie.

'Fair's fair,' said Pistol-Man as Avalon went into the kitchen with the plate, giving Vera a broad grin as he went. 'I cook for him, but he must wash up. That's only fair, isn't it? We both share the work.'

'What happened to his mum?' Vera couldn't help asking. Pistol-Man gave an exasperated sort of sigh and shook his head:

'She left,' he said, sitting back down in his chair. 'She was a virgin when I met her, so I don't know why I went with her because I don't like virgins,' he said candidly. 'We lived in a little room in Stoke Newington. I was working as a cutter – you know – cloth – cutting cloth. Avalon was seventeen months old. She left on a Friday. Well, you know how horrible Fridays are.' He opened his arms wide as if to emphasise the horribleness of Fridays. 'You've been working all week and you're tired and you're looking forward to the weekend. Anyway, I came home and found a note stuck on the paraffin heater saying she'd gone. The baby was all pissed up in his cot. And that was that.' He frowned as though it was still a puzzle to him. 'Maybe I was a bit of a tyrant,' he said regretfully. 'But I didn't beat her or anything,' he added hastily. 'It was just that when I wanted something done, I wanted it done properly. I wanted it done the right way.' Vera could see how the man could be bossy, cantankerous even. He continued with an expression of bewildered anguish on his face:

'It's because I want people to make progress. I want things to be better. Even with him,' he gestured towards Avalon who had gone into the bathroom, 'I want him to be somebody.' He spoke with a burst of energy, enthusiasm and hope. 'I want him to be something. He can't hear and he can't speak much but I want him to be the best he can. To be his own person.' He got up and pointed out of the window. 'That's why I've let the grass grow like that.' Vera looked to where he was pointing. Outside, the grass had run wild, nearly waist-high, in the small garden. 'The neighbours keep telling me I must cut it, but it's more interesting for him like that. There's lots of things he can discover in that grass: butterflies and worms, snails and caterpillars and insects with long legs, lots of things. He can hide in it and imagine things. It's more of an adventure for him like that.'

Avalon came in and took his father by both forearms, then he bared his teeth at him.

'Yes. That's all right,' said Pistol-Man. He turned to Vera, a little shame-faced, to explain. 'I make him do that because he didn't used to brush his teeth properly. I should stop him doing that really,' he said. 'He's too old for that now. Would you like to see his drawing? He's talented. Maybe he'll get trained one day.'

He ushered Vera into the boy's bedroom. It was small and pokey. Two big wardrobes dwarfed the single bed. Over the head of the bed was a picture of Superman. On the other wall was Avalon's drawing of Elvis Presley. Vera smiled and nodded at Avalon in appreciation. Immediately, the boy jumped on the bed and tried to pull down a big folder from the top of the wardrobe, indicating that he wanted to give her all the drawings he had ever done.

'She don't want all those, silly,' said Pistol-Man. He opened the wardrobe. Inside were half a drum-kit and a battered electric guitar. 'Those are my instruments,' he said proudly. 'I'll show you my room.'

The three of them peeked into his room. Vera was made shy by the sight of his double bed, neatly made up with a plain coverlet. She glanced quickly round. On a shelf was another photograph of Avalon with two schoolfriends. There was not much else in the room. She backed out. They returned to the living-room.

'I've got to go now,' she said.

'You're shooting off then,' said Pistol-Man. In his eagerness to do what she wanted he almost ran her out of the front door.

'Call in any time you want,' he said. 'We're always in from about six o'clock. Thanks again for the lift.'

'Bye . . . Bye,' said Avalon.

Vera waved goodbye. It had stopped raining. As she drove through the cramped streets an immense and irreparable sense of loss overwhelmed her for the island where she had once lived with its whispering seas and the sound of women's voices in the soft night air, dripping slowly and unevenly like molasses; for the people she had once known.

Back in his flat, Pistol-Man slapped himself on the forehead:

'Oh no! I forgot to ask her her name.' Avalon pulled a face of commiseration. 'Not that it matters.' Pistol-Man no longer thought about women because of his dedication to the boy.

'Did you like her?' asked Pistol-Man. Avalon, his eyes shining, put his hands on his lips and then on his heart. He went back to his drawing on the floor. Pistol-Man sat on the settee and opened another can of lager. He felt good. He felt warm inside. Tomorrow, he decided, he would hoover the carpet and give the whole place a good clean-up. What luck, he thought, to get a lift home on a wet afternoon like that.

Suddenly, he leant forward and grasped his son by the arm to attract his attention. He spoke in sign language only:

'You see!' he said to the child who looked intently at him. 'Good things do happen.'

ABOUT THAT TWO POUNDS, MRS PARRISH

When Lily Johnson opened her front door, the woman on the doorstep was already smiling at her. The stranger's eyes, set deep in a broad forehead, made Lily uncomfortable. They looked at her too directly. Altogether, the woman looked like a brown plant that had sprung up on her doorstep. A stained, fawn mackintosh hung loose, half-covering some dun-coloured slacks and an old, yellowish sweater. At her side stood a child with orange hair and green eyes who looked as if he had been fed on too much milk. From her accent, Lily knew the woman was posh.

Across the street, Mrs O'Sullivan stood staring at the two women on Lily's doorstep, her head cocked to one side. Two weeks ago when Lily and her husband rented the house opposite, Mrs O'Sullivan had been the first to call, offering assistance, dropping packages, her brown eyes anxious and curious, her cheap purple coat flapping open, her lop-sided features in a permanent gawp. Since then, Lily had seen her several times in the street, swaying from side to side as she walked, as if she were trying to catch somebody's scent. Now, Lily's attention was distracted from the well-spoken stranger because, over the woman's shoulder, she could see Mrs O'Sullivan staring at them. She leaned sideways and gave Mrs O'Sullivan a small wave to indicate that she had caught her spying. As if released from a spell, Mrs O'Sullivan resumed motion, picked up a bottle of milk from the doorstep and retreated inside her terraced house.

'So, if you'd like to bring her up to play . . .' The woman was inviting Lily to bring her daughter, Gloria, to play with the orange-haired boy. They lived in the big white house on the corner. The boy stared down the street as if none of this had anything to do with him.

'That's so kind.' Lily was flustered. 'I'll fetch her up later.'

Blasted nuisance, thought Lily as she shut the door. She picked her way past the tea-chests in the dark passage and went into the back room that adjoined the tiny, cold scullery. In the back parlour, her sister Ruby's broad frame balanced skew-whiff on the window-sill, arms outstretched as if to a sun-god. Between her hands drooped a tape measure.

'Well, whadderyerknow.' Lily whispered as if the visitor could still hear them. 'That was the woman from the white house. What a sight! You'd never think she was a doctor's wife in a million years. At least, that Irish woman over the road told me the house on the corner was a doctor's house. Dirty old trousers she had on.'

'Ooooooooer.' Ruby shifted her weight to reach the other side of the window frame. The garish colours and unmatching patterns of her blouse and skirt zig-zagged and clashed like tropical fish fighting in an aquarium. A petticoat hung way below her cotton skirt. Lily observed it critically:

'That petticoat needs shortening.'

Lily sat at the table. She wore a floral, crêpe frock and old white sandals. Her dark hair was pinned in sausage curls round her head and held in place by a hairnet. Hooded lids drooped over eyes the same colour as the irises in the back yard. She picked out a pea with a maggot in it from the basin and tossed it in the paper bag with the rest of the pods. It annoyed her that Ruby was not that impressed by the caller:

'Mind you, she had a lovely way of talking. I'll bet their place is nice inside.' Her eyes screwed up with cunning. 'I think I will pop up later and 'ave a snoop.'

Ruby tried to disregard her sister's snobbery. Lily was the only one of the family with pretensions. When the others teased her about it she would turn and retort, 'You can always stoop and pick up nuffin!'

'Toreador, bom bom ti bom ti bom,' Ruby sang in tune with the radio as she lowered her bulk to the ground. 'That's that done!' She sat in the low chair beneath the window, sipping at her lukewarm tea, trying to judge how much weight Lily had lost since the operation. Her sister's skin looked clear but pale:

'Lily's a good name for you. You look like a bloody lily.'

'Don't be so daft.' Lily threw a scornful look at her sister. 'And I'm not having you come over here day after day unless you let me give you your fares.'

'Don't be so barmy. It's only a couple of bob. What's a couple of bob?'

'It's a couple of bob,' said Lily firmly. She reached in her bag and took out the rough leather purse she'd made at evening classes. The teacher had cut out the shape and punched the holes in it and Lily had bound it together with brown plastic. Then the teacher had stamped the stud on the front. Lily took from it a two shilling piece. She placed it on the table as though she were making a careful chess move.

'Put that back. What are sisters for if they can't help each other out?' said Ruby.

Lily returned the money to her purse:

'What in God's world would I do without you, Ruby?' She studied the floor. 'What do you think of this lino? I dunno if I'm struck. D'you think he'll mind it being red?'

Ruby was putting on her make-up without looking in a mirror. She imagined where her eyebrows used to be – in much the same place as Marlene Dietrich's – and then ran the eyebrow pencil over her forehead. She guessed roughly where her lips were, wielding the lipstick in close approximation to their shape and patted her face with a powder puff until the powder drifted into orange sand-dunes beneath her cheek bones.

Four weeks earlier, Lily had been in hospital with peritonitis. She examined her arms:

'I've got thin everywhere except these bloody arms. A horse would be proud of one of these arms for a leg. Wish I had refined arms.'

The back door rattled. The sisters semaphored surprise to each other with their eyebrows and mouths.

'That's never school over, is it?' asked Lily.

Gloria hopped up the steps from the scullery into the back parlour. One plait was coming undone and she had the remains of a black eye from fighting with the dentist to stop the gas mask being put over her face. Ruby held out her arms like a colourful parrot and Gloria swooped into them, breathing in a cloud of

Devonshire Violet talcum powder. Aunty Ruby felt like a marshmallow.

'Don't take that coat off,' said Lily. 'You're going to play with someone up the road.'

'But I wanna stick me transfers on me arm.' Gloria jutted out her pale, fierce little face.

'You can do that after.' Lily held the hairpins in her mouth as she fastened a loose strand of hair. Ruby glanced in the mirror to fix her felt hat at a more jaunty angle. As the two sisters and the child sauntered up the hill, Mrs O'Sullivan's curtain moved.

The inside of the doctor's house astonished Lily. The floor of the large, airy living room was bare – dark, polished wooden boards. French windows looked out onto a long, unkempt garden. Half-way down the room was a baby grand piano and in the corner stood a display cabinet full of red, black and gold-patterned chinaware. There were no ornaments on the mantelpiece. There were no curtains at the windows. The only furniture in the room was a down-at-heel settee and an ancient, ungainly armchair. Lily stood in the centre of the room. The spaciousness of it made her feel agoraphobic. The room was too full of light. She became self-conscious. Her recent visitor leaned with her back to the fireplace, heels resting on the fireguard. Lily noticed that she wore plimsolls. But they must have money, thought Lily. It all seemed peculiar. She had thought there would be carpets.

Perched on the edge of the settee was another woman, a woman who seemed altogether a more suitable occupant for a doctor's house. Mrs Parrish. Mrs Parrish stirred a cup of tea with a small silver spoon. Immediately, Lily was reminded of the Duchess of Windsor. Her silhouette was etched sharply against the light from the French windows. On her head was a neat, black hat with a spotted veil. Protruding from one side of the hat was a piece of stiffened felt the shape of a crow's tail feathers. Immaculate was the word that came to Lily's mind as they were introduced.

'Does your husband have his surgery in this house?' Lily enquired politely.

'Oh, I'm the doctor,' laughed the woman, still in her brown raincoat.

Lily suffered an attack of violent social vertigo. What a blunder. But how on earth was she supposed to know? – the blasted woman dressed as though she kept chickens. The colour rose in Lily's cheeks. Dr Bartholomew, as she had turned out to be, appeared not to notice.

'In fact, Mrs Parrish's husband and I were medical students together. He has a surgery further up the hill. I work in the Public Health department.'

'How nice it must be to have brains,' stammered Lily.

Mrs Parrish had turned her head and was smiling at her. Her cheeks were puffy. For a second she reminded Lily of a python.

Outside in the garden, the orange-haired boy had been transformed into a maniac. He had Gloria pinned to the wall with a piece of fence beneath her ribs and was pushing as hard as he could with a fixed grimace. They both were silent. When she could barely breathe, Gloria spoke:

'My dad is secetary to the Queen.'

The boy suddenly dropped the piece of fence and stomped off down the path, awkwardly as if he was wearing frogman's flippers, yelling, 'YAH. YAH. YAH. YAH.'

Dr Bartholomew looked at her watch: 'I have to leave for a Labour Party meeting.'

Every turn of the conversation left Lily more confused. Now the posh-sounding doctor appeared to be a supporter of the working man. Lily thanked God that she had had peritonitis. At least that was something medical to talk about, although Mrs Parrish, an obviously superior woman, had topped her by having had cancer and a miracle cure.

Lily's head was buzzing as she and Gloria walked home. Dr Bartholomew's deep inset eyes reminded Lily of the green Mikon Man in Gloria's comic books. Perhaps she was in touch with the other side. Or had fits. Mrs Parrish was another kettle of fish. Mrs Parrish was how Lily would like to be.

'Not a piece of carpet on the floor. Not a shred.'

Lily was shouting above the spitting of sausages in the pan as she stood by the stove in the dilapidated scullery. George

Johnson sat quietly at the table waiting for his supper, his finger-nails still dirty from work at the power station although he had scrubbed his hands. Gloria bobbed up and down in front of the mirror putting beetroot juice on her lips for lipstick.

'There was not.' Lily continued as if some invisible person had contradicted her. 'Not one stitch. Bare boards. No rugs. Nothing. Not even a mat to brighten the place up. She's not a proper doctor with a surgery. She goes round schools or something. That Mrs Parrish is a lovely woman. She had one of those miracle cures for cancer. She was very ill and then all her genes got together and her blood changed and she got better.'

Lily watched George as he ate. Strands of greasy, toffee-coloured hair hung over his forehead as he shovelled the food into his mouth. She wondered what it would be like to be sitting opposite Dr Parrish. There would probably be a glass of sherry, a white linen tablecloth and perhaps a silver entrée dish with some weird vegetable like broccoli.

She pinned up Gloria's plaits and put her in the tin bath in front of the Ideal boiler. Gloria kept her left arm sticking out so as not to let the transfers wash off. Soap turned the water milky. The side of the bath nearest to the fire was getting too hot. Gloria clung to the other side:

'What do you want f'yer birthday, mum?' she asked.

'I want a packet of hairpins and a hairnet. That's what I want more than anything else in God's world.' Lily winked at George who took out his wallet.

' 'Ere Lil. Something for y'birthday.' He pressed the money into her hand and squeezed it so tight she couldn't tell how much was there. She looked down. Two pounds.

'Oh you shouldn't't've.' George looked embarrassed so Lily changed the subject.

'What do you think to this red lino?'

'Makes the place look like a slaughterhouse,' said George.

That night, Lily turned away from her husband's body which was burning hot as he slept, like the furnaces he stoked all day, and moved to the cool edge of the bed. Once asleep, she dreamed she was standing in the middle of a road on top of a hill. She was holding with difficulty the entire front section of an ambulance. Speeding towards her, its emergency bell ringing, was an ambulance with no front. She knew she was supposed to fit the front on as it reached her. As the white vehicle loomed towards her she stepped forward and fitted the missing section into position. As she did so, the top of the ambulance flew open and out sprang Mrs Parrish, like a Jack-in-the-Box, swinging backwards and forwards and smiling bravely.

The next day, Lily collected Gloria from school and they went straight to look in the window of Bon Marché Department Store which was already displaying autumn fashions. On one of the models was a red woollen coat with a trim belt to match and a snazzy black astrakhan collar. FOXY QUEEN COAT shouted the label. Two pounds ten shillings. Lily calculated that with the birthday money and what she would be able to save from the housekeeping she could afford it. They had told her at the hospital that she must not return to waitressing in the café for at least three months, but she should be able to get the extra ten shillings although it would mean Gloria doing without the patent leather shoes she wanted. A gust of hot wind blew grit into Gloria's eye. Lily spat on her handkerchief and got it out. Then the two of them walked down Coldharbour Lane to the Golden Domes cinema where Gloria had lost her gloves the week before. Lily reckoned she couldn't last the winter without a coat.

'They were white cotton gloves with a strawberry pattern on them like little hearts. I dunno how she lost them. They were threaded on a bit of elastic through her coat.' Lily was yelling through the plastic front of the kiosk to a hunch-back woman with thick pebble glasses who sat in a mountain of sweets, cigarettes and Kia-Ora orange juice. Lily threw a warning look at Gloria who was walking around in circles pretending she had a club foot. The woman opened a couple of drawers half-heartedly and shook her head.

'You are a pest,' said Lily outside the cinema. And suddenly, she spotted Mrs Parrish. Mrs Parrish stood at the bus stop across the road. She wore a navy-blue linen dress with a red and white striped collar. As she mounted the bus the dress fluttered like a spruce naval flag. Lily took Gloria into the greengrocer's. It smelled of wood and old vegetables. All the women in there looked like the vegetables they were buying. One woman had the face of a parsnip, etched with the same fine parallel lines; another had a face as bland and thoughtless as a cabbage; a third stood there in a sad, beetroot-coloured coat. Once, in Harrods, Lily had seen women expensively packaged like boxes of Swiss chocolates or elegantly wrapped cakes; women with complexions like the waxed fruits in the Food Hall; women who walked in their own distinctive cloud of perfume. Mrs Parrish is a bit like that, she thought.

Altogether, Lily's head was so full of Mrs Parrish that it seemed the most natural thing in the world when, the next day, Mrs Parrish stood on Lily's doorstep:

'I am most dreadfully sorry to ask you, but the bank has shut and I wondered if you could possibly lend me a couple of pounds. I could let you have it back on Monday as soon as the banks open again. I should be so grateful.'

Lily almost ran to the back room for the two pounds she had hidden behind one of the plates on the dresser. What a bit of luck! Normally she would never have that sort of cash to spare.

'I don't know how to thank you.' Mrs Parrish's eyes were both bright and dull at the same time, as if they had been boiled.

'Whenever you're ready. No rush.' Lily rapped Gloria on the head. Gloria had ducked under her mother's loosened apron and was poking her head out of the top like a kangaroo in a pouch. The two women exchanged tiny, ladylike waves.

On Monday Lily tidied the front room. She picked the best of the lupins from the back yard and arranged them in two vases. Then she baked a tray of rock cakes. She put them in the front room covered with a damp cloth so they would not dry out. Then she waited. Mrs Parrish did not come. Gloria came home from school and ate half the rock cakes. George arrived home from work. She won't come this late, thought Lily. She'll come tomorrow.

Mrs Parrish did not appear on the Tuesday either. Lily became concerned in case she was ill again. She began to fret and snap at Gloria. Surely Mrs Parrish couldn't have forgotten. Two pounds was too much to forget. And then, a few days later, as if the sun had come out, Lily caught sight of the familiar trim figure at the bus stop. Lily twisted the handles of her shopping bag nervously:

'Oh excuse me, Mrs Parrish. I was wondering if you could give me that two pounds back.' She nearly added 'I'm a bit short' and then didn't.

'I'm so sorry. I haven't got it on me at the moment. I'll drop it through your letter-box.'

Mrs Parrish's puffy cheeks rose in an inscrutably polite smile. Relief flooded Lily.

For the next week or so, every time the letter-box rattled Lily darted to the door. Sometimes she thought she'd heard it rattle when it hadn't and she would find herself in the dark passageway staring disappointedly at the doormat. The whole business puzzled her. Finally, she plucked up courage to call on Dr Bartholomew.

The doctor opened the door. Her frank smile put Lily at ease. From the back of the house came the sound of children playing.

'I just called because I haven't seen Mrs Parrish lately and I was a bit worried in case she was ill again.'

'On no, she's fine. In fact, she and her husband had dinner with us last night.' Dr Bartholomew bent to restrain the over-friendly mongrel dog.

'I'm so glad,' said Lily and hesitated. 'Actually she owes me a little money.'

'Really?' Dr Bartholomew laughed. 'As a matter of fact I think she owes me some too. I'll remind her if I see her before they go away. They go to Whitstable every year for the summer.'

'How nice,' said Lily. 'Where the oysters come from,' she added vaguely.

All summer long the sky was blue and cloudless. Twice, Lily walked all the way up the hill to the Parrishes' house. She peered down the gravel drive trying to catch any sign of life through the latticed windows. Dr Parrish's car was not in the drive. The house seemed deserted.

Lily brooded ceaselessly over the two pounds. She tried to finish sewing a curtain for the front of the orange-box that was to be Gloria's bedside table but she couldn't settle to it. George offered her the money to take Gloria to Southend for the weekend. Consumed with guilt and not able to tell him about it, she refused. Sometimes she thought she would never see the money again. The thought made her sick.

One morning, however, she awoke filled with a sort of wild hilarity. She sat up in the high double bed that nearly filled the room and could not imagine what she had been worrying about. Soon the Parrishes would be back from their holidays and then she would undoubtedly get the money back. George had gone to work. She threw back the sheets and the thin eiderdown. Feeling elated, she dressed and dabbed some perfume the colour of medicine behind her ears. School holidays ended the next day.

'Gloria,' she called down the stairs, 'how about going to Lyon's for a treat?'

In the cool gloom of Lyon's Corner House, Lily and Gloria sat on fixed seats at a marble-topped table. Gloria drank her strawberry milk-shake slowly through a straw. Lily ate a Kunzle cake. Mrs O'Sullivan lumbered towards them, tray in hand, her bags bumping against her thighs. As she put her tray on their table she knocked over the dregs of an uncollected cup of tea.

'Hello, dear. How are you?' She started to chase her scoop of chocolate ice-cream round the shiny pewter bowl. Lily watched as her mouth worked open and shut like a large purple sea-anemone. 'I saw that Mrs Parrish call on you a while back. I hope you didn't lend her any money.'

'What do you mean?' She looked anxiously at Mrs O'Sullivan.

'You'll never see sight nor sound of it again if you did. She's borrowed bits and pieces from everybody in the neighbourhood. I meant to warn you.'

Lily's skin prickled up her arms and across the back of her neck as if she had been stung by a Portuguese Man o' War:

'Oh, it was nothing like that. It was just a social call.'

'Just as well, dear. Be warned.'

'But why should she do that? They must have money.'

'I dunno, dear. Nobody knows anybody,' she said darkly. 'Not a soul in this world knows what goes on in somebody else's head. Not a soul.'

Mrs O'Sullivan made her way out, squeezing between tables, holding her bags up in the air to prevent them knocking over people's cups and saucers and biffing people on the head with them as a result:

'Sorry, dear. Excuse me, dear. Sorry, dear.'

Lily sat motionless. The huge restaurant seemed to have grown darker. Dimly she heard the steely clatter and clash of cutlery being collected. It sounded like the distant din of a great battlefield. Two women pushing trolleys of dirty cups and plates appeared to be moving with urgency as if they were nurses in a field hospital. Lily felt faint.

'Let's go,' she said to Gloria.

Autumn came fiercely and with it a biting east wind. The days grew shorter. There was no sign of Mrs Parrish. Lily no longer saw her at bus stops or at the shops. She's changed her haunts to avoid me, thought Lily grimly. And indeed she had. Once Lily spotted her and trailed her all the way to Herne Hill, but just as she called out to her, Mrs Parrish hailed a taxi and sailed off in it leaving Lily to walk home. She began to feel dragging pains in her stomach. Another time, Lily saw the oldest Parrish boy in the street, wearing a pale blue cap that did not belong to any of the schools in the neighbourhood:

'Excuse me, I'm Mrs Johnson. I wonder if you would be so kind as to tell your mother I'm still waiting for her to call on me.'

'Certainly,' replied the mystified youth with overlapping front teeth.

Lily made up her mind to go to the Parrishes' house and confront the woman. She told George she was going to post a letter. The lights were on in the front of the house. Lily could see a standard lamp behind a chintz-covered sofa. Then it occurred to her that Dr Parrish might answer the door and she would not know what to say. Defeated, she turned and went home. Over the next few weeks she began to dust the window-sill in the front room again and again although it was perfectly clean. Sometimes she just sat all afternoon and watched the rain measling the window panes. And then, one night, George found Lily struggling up the stairs with a full coal scuttle.

'Where the 'ell are you goin' with that?' He was half-laughing at the bottom of the stairs. Lily stared at the scuttle in disbelief. She had mistaken it for her handbag. She tried to laugh it off but she was shocked.

The incident with the coal scuttle decided her. She must put the two pounds out of her mind. No point in going barmy.

She made herself a cup of tea, lit the boiler and nearly dozed off in the back parlour. It was getting dark. Drum-rolls of rain beat against the window lashing the few grape hyacinths left upstanding in the window-box. An artist, seeing Lily just then, would have wanted to paint her. She sat in the low chair, head slightly on one side, a strand of brown hair coiled around her neck. The milky skin of her arms showed up in the darkened room. Her eyes, under half-closed lids expressed a gentle self-mockery. It was late. She jerked herself awake. There was just time to go and buy supper before the shops shut. These days she waited until it grew dark before going shopping. She put newspaper under her thin coat to keep out the wind and after dark there was less likelihood of somebody catching sight of it. She wrapped several sheets of old newspaper round her body and tied them firmly round the waist with strands of strong wool. Like a flipping Christmas cracker, she laughed to herself. She put on a cardigan and slid her arms in the sleeves of her raincoat.

Gusts of icy rain made her catch her breath as she hurried up the street. She turned the corner and lowered her head against the full blast of the wind. Her shoes began to let water. On the main street she kept to the inside of the pavement so as not to be further drenched with spray by passing cars. Glancing behind her she was thankful to see the lights of an approaching bus. She looked ahead to see if she would reach the bus stop in time. Standing there under a black umbrella was Mrs Parrish. Lily began to run:

'Mrs Parrish. Mrs Parrish.'

Cars hissed by on the wet road. Mrs Parrish was lowering her umbrella in readiness to board the bus. She seemed to be staring curiously at Lily. Lily looked down. Sheets of sodden newspaper had slipped from under her coat and were falling to the ground.

She tried to kick one away from round her ankle as she ran. 'Sod the bloody newspaper,' she muttered to herself. 'I want my money back.'

'I want my money back.' She screamed out loud, the wind snatching the words away and twisting them out of recognition behind her back. The bus overtook Lily. Inside it looked warm and bright and cheerful. Mrs Parrish mounted the bus. Lily's left foot skidded on leaves and wet paper. The glistening pavement rose sharply at an angle and cracked her on the forehead. Something seemed to snap and unravel in her stomach. She lay dazed, unable to tell whether it was rain or blood that wetted her forehead. Her coat had burst open revealing the remains of the newspaper underneath but she was too weak to try and hide it. Rain swept over her like a yard brush. The solid block of pain in her abdomen paralysed her legs. The conductor had stopped the bus ten yards further on. He ran back to her:

'All right, missis?' He helped her to her feet. Lily could barely speak:

'I'll be all right. I'm only round the corner.' As the bus drew away she could see the silhouette of Mrs Parrish's crow black hat. She dragged herself home.

When Gloria arrived home from her tap-dancing class the house was in darkness. She heard a noise upstairs and found Lily kneeling on the floor of the toilet, resting her head against the china bowl between bouts of vomiting. Gloria helped her to bed, then fetched the pail, ran some water into it and added a few drops of Dettol until the water went cloudy. She put it by the bed and wiped Lily's face with a damp flannel. Lily patted her hand. At seven o'clock George came home. Gloria tried to make him some baked beans on toast. At intervals during the evening, Gloria would go up and empty the bucket, putting fresh Dettol and water in it. One time she came downstairs and said:

'There's blood in the bucket.'

George stood in the doorway of the bedroom:

'Dr Parrish is here to see you.'

Lily was dimly aware of a heavy, well-built man who breathed heavily as he bent to examine her, his stiff white collar biting into his red neck. She nodded or shook her head exhaustedly in response to his questions. George looked humbly attentive from the doorway. Gloria had been sent to find Dr Bartholomew who arrived and stood on the cramped landing. Gloria listened to both her and Dr Parrish in turn as they spoke. 'Twisted intestine. Adhesions? Serious. Foecal vomit.'

Gloria stood at the top of the stairs holding on to the banisters feeling solemn and important as the ambulance men tried to manoeuvre the stretcher down the narrow stairs. One of the men bent to hear what Lily was trying to say. She whispered:

'Don't ring the ambulance bell. I hate that Mrs O'Sullivan. She's so nosy.'

'I'm jacking,' said McGregor.

It was ten o'clock in the morning. The other scaffolder hadn't turned up. It had taken him half an hour to unload the freezing scaffolding tubes from the lorry, the ringing clang of tube against tube increasingly setting his teeth on edge. That done, he set about emptying the lorry of piles of metal fittings so that the driver could get away. He banged on the side of the cab. The driver raised his thumb and backed the vehicle off the site. McGregor looked up at a sky laden with snow. Then he examined the palms of his hands. They were a shiny, raw pink where the frozen metal had taken off the first layer of skin. They burned him. Flexing his hands, he walked over to the foot of the unfinished, eight-storey building and began to base out the scaffold. On his own, he erected the first level, using the heavy, twenty-one foot tubes as uprights. With deft, experienced twists of the podger on the metal nuts, he fastened the four foot tubes to the uprights, some slantwise and some horizontally so that they reached the wall. One by one, he heaved the wooden planks from the pile at the foot of the wall and laid them out along the structure. Then he decided to quit the job and go drinking.

'I said I'm jacking,' shouted McGregor to the site foreman, trying to make himself heard over the grinding roar of the cement-mixer. The foreman motioned to the hod-carrier, showing him where the bricks were to go. Then he turned to McGregor with drooping shoulders:

'What's up, Jock?' Steam issued from his mouth.

'You can stick your fucking job up your fucking arse.'

McGregor grinned. 'I'm jacking.' The foreman looked pained for a minute and then shrugged:

'Go and tell them at the site office. Tell them to phone head office and send me down two more scaffolders.'

McGregor went over and unhitched his jacket from where it hung on the end of a piece of scaffolding. He undid his belt with a mounting sense of freedom and took off the leather frogs which held his half-inch Whitworth spanner and the seven-sixteenth A.F. He chucked the podger and the spanners into his canvas tool-bag and walked over the icy, rutted ground to the portocabin by the gates. He began to whistle.

Inside the portacabin, the air was fuggy from the calor gas heater. Mr Oates, the site manager, was on the telephone at a desk littered with papers. Pinned to a noticeboard near the door was a letter from a Mrs Kathleen Doherty, written in a loopy scrawl, thanking the men for the collection after her husband's accident. McGregor read it idly as he waited. Mr Oates put down the telephone. A cigarette with long ash burned between his fingers. White hair with nicotine yellow streaks lay stiffly on either side of his head like bird wings. He looked at McGregor enquiringly.

'I'm away,' said McGregor. 'Just phone the office and tell them to make up me cards and me wage packet. I'm on me way over to get them now.'

'It's only ten o'clock. Can't you finish the morning?'

'No. I'm away now. Sammy says to tell you to ask for two more scaffolders.' McGregor turned to leave.

'What's your name?' asked Mr Oates, wearily.

'Jock the Jacker.' McGregor gave a wry smile. 'Mac. McGregor,' he said as he left. He walked through the site gates. On the street, he took a deep breath and straightened his shoulders. Rows of mean, secretive, terraced houses stretched down the road in front of him. McGregor paused to inspect the contents of his pocket. Forty pence. He set off at a brisk pace to walk the two miles to the main office. Unexpectedly, the day felt full of promise.

'Mr McGregor, is it?' The dumpy girl in a brown sweater greeted him from the cashier's desk in the construction company's main office.

'Ay. That's it.'

She reached in the drawer and pulled out a buff wage packet and his cards:

'We've deducted the twenty pound sub. There's five weeks' holiday stamps on your holiday card and you can pick up the week in hand next Thursday. OK?'

The wage register was pushed across the desk and he signed it.

'Don't forget I done three hours this morning,' McGregor reminded her.

'Well that won't be due until the Thursday after next. You see today's Thursday and the work up until today, that's your week in hand, gets paid next Thursday, but any work you do today doesn't get paid till the Thursday after that. OK?'

McGregor felt a tightening in the muscles of his neck.

'Thanks,' he said. He took the wage packet and went.

At eleven o'clock precisely, the publican unlocked the doors of his Fulham pub and McGregor stepped over the threshold into the quiet, gloomy interior. The low moan of a hoover came from somewhere over his head. Sleepily, the publican made his way behind the bar.

'Gi'us a double scotch there, please,' said McGregor.

McGregor's drinking habit ran to a formula; two whiskies in quick succession while he stood at the bar and then straight out and onto the next pub. By the time he reached the fourth one it was snowing. He was somewhere in the back streets of Chelsea. The whisky had begun to do its work, cutting a warm channel through the centre of his body. For the first time, he relaxed enough to take stock of his surroundings. The pub appeared to be empty. Then he caught sight of an old man seated round the corner, his figure half-eaten up by shadows:

'Can I get you something there?' he called across to the old man. The man's head moved a little:

'Half a pint, thank you.' The voice was cracked and thin. McGregor ordered a scotch for himself and a beer for the man. They sat in silence for a while. The pensioner spilled his beer as he sipped it. He had eyes that watered permanently, the colour of faded bluebells:

'You a soldier?' he asked.

'I was once,' replied McGregor. 'I was slung out. Retention

Undesirable in the Interest of Her Majesty's Services.' He delivered the words with a flourish as if they were poetry. And laughed.

'I was in Spain,' said the man.

'Oh yes?' McGregor seemed interested.

'I fought with the International Brigade in the Spanish Civil War.'

'Is that a fact?' McGregor waited. The old man leaned forward into a shaft of dull light from the window. McGregor saw motes of dust dancing down the light onto the amber liquid in the glass.

'I was with them in Madrid in 1936. I saw such things. Such terrible things.' He wiped his chin with his checked scarf. 'When I came back to England I had to tell everybody what I had seen. For thirty years, every Sunday, I took, a soap-box in Hyde Park Corner and I told what I had seen to anybody who would listen. I never missed a Sunday for thirty years. And then I stopped.' He leaned back into the shadows. McGregor finished his drink. The old man's glass was still nearly full.

'Will I get you another?' McGregor asked. But the old man had closed up in the darkness like a flower in the night. A restlessness overcame McGregor and he stood up:

'Good luck, then.'

'And you, sir,' came the voice from the invisible man.

Flakes of wet snow came to rest on McGregor's eyelashes as he walked with the urgency of a man not knowing where he is going.

An hour later, poised between conviviality and violence, McGregor stood in a bar crowded with lunch-time drinkers. He was locked in intense conversation with the father of a baby with no future, a pale young man with red hair. The young father's lack of optimism was depressing him:

'How old did you say the baby was?' asked McGregor. The man consulted his watch.

'Eight and a half hours old,' he said dejectedly. 'He'll never get a home of his own, poor little blighter. Look how many homeless there are.'

McGregor became determined to raise the man's spirits. It was like pushing an enormous boulder uphill.

'And there's no jobs,' said the man. 'He'll never get a job. That's for sure. No chance.'

McGregor tried harder.

'Och, I dunno. You've got a wee boy. Kids are clever these days. They understand computers. They go to college and all sorts of strange things.'

'Only if they've got money.'

McGregor's face was flushed. He tried again.

'They get grants. They can do anything.'

Suspended in a corner of the bar was a television set with the sound turned down, showing images of soliders chasing and firing on people somewhere in the Middle East. McGregor hoped the young man wouldn't see it.

'D'you reckon?' The red-haired man looked faintly hopeful. McGregor began to sweat:

'Jesus. Kids are magic these days. They speak out. They don't put up with any shit.' Somewhere in the back of his brain, McGregor knew that if the man slipped back into despondency, he would be obliged to punch him off his stool.

'Maybe you're right,' said the man, reluctantly.

McGregor's voice rose above the buzz of conversation around him as he made a final effort:

'Of course I'm fucking right. Kids have got everything. I wish I was nine hours old. All snuggly and comfy. I wish I was a fucking kid. And another thing. Kids love music. He'll be a musician. That's what's going to happen. He's going to be a great musician. They all play in bands. They make terrific music.'

McGregor held his breath.

'Yeah. You're right, I suppose.' The man managed a wan grin.

'Right y'are then,' said McGregor, triumphantly.

The future of the child assured and the man saved from injury, McGregor made to leave. He drained the remains of his whisky:

'Slainte Mhath,' he said in Gaelic.

The high street looked familiar but he did not recognise it. A lighted bus drew up beside him like an invitation and he stepped onto it.

The upper deck of the bus was brightly lit. Stale smoke and a litter of cigarette ends on the floor gave it the bleakly cheerful air of a public bar that had unexpectedly taken to travelling through the dark afternoon. McGregor sat bolt upright in the back seat. The beginnings of a transformation were taking place. His hands gripped the rail in front of him as if he were on the Big Wheel of a funfair. One blazing green eye was wide open, staring ahead with fierce energy, the other was lazily half open like that of a waking child. Faint streaks of mud from the morning's work still decorated his face. Dried mud stiffened his jeans. Somewhere along the way, his jacket had taken off on a journey of its own. The same fine dusting of sand and cement that covered his navy-blue polo-neck sweater caused his hair to stick up in pointed, uneven spikes. Here and there in the spikes sat spangles of snow. Altogether, he looked like one of those creatures that has lain immobile in mud-flats for the duration of a drought waiting for the rains to come in order to return to life.

The wide-open eye focused with dislike on the passengers ahead of him. Suddenly, his expression changed. A look of intense delight spread over his face. His shoulders moved from side to side and he tapped his feet as he whistled the tune of 'A Hundred Pipers an a' an a' '. He sang the words out, savouring each one, on his face an expression of menacing bliss. The passengers remained silent. No one looked at him. McGregor finished the song and looked expectantly round the bus. The look twisted into a sneer:

'You're all dead people,' he shouted.

The man in front of him stared deliberately out of the window. McGregor rose to his feet and held onto the rail to steady himself:

'What would you say if I said "Let's all get off the bus and light a big bonfire in the street"?' he enquired, enthusiastically.

There was no response. Two women at the front of the bus continued to talk, one of them in a voice as clear as a bell in winter.

'How about setting fire to the bus?' he suggested. 'How about giving it a Viking's funeral?'

No one responded. Attracted by the only sign of life, the conversation at the other end of the bus, McGregor stepped carefully down the centre aisle like a seaman navigating the narrow passageway of a rolling ship. With a jerk, he sat down in the empty front seat next to the two women:

'Excuse me, lady.' He spoke in the dangerously polite tones of the extremely drunk. The crippled woman with the shining face pulled her lame leg in towards her. The leg, much shorter than the other one, was fitted with a contraption of metal and leather, terminating in a shiny, black, surgical boot that seemed too solid to contain a foot.

'Never mind the leg, lady. Legs aren't important. What happened to your leg, anyway?'

The woman, unruffled by the question, began to give the history of her malformed foot. Her rational explanation and unwavering gaze horrified McGregor. He shut his eyes. When he opened them again, the woman had turned back to her friend and was discussing the essay she had to write on Jane Austen for her evening class.

'A man's a man for a' that,' he mumbled, attempting to roll himself a cigarette from his tobacco tin as the bus swayed. He lit the cigarette and fished out the brown pay packet from his pocket. He took out the long, thin wage-slip:

'Forty-eight pounds fucking emergency TAX.' He bellowed the last word. 'I've been mugged by the government.' He scrumpled up the paper and flung it down. Annoyed by the lack of impact, he ground the paper serpent into the ridged floor with his foot. Suddenly, his limbs turned to lead and a great weariness took hold of him:

'Mud. Cold. Shit. Wind. Steel. Rain. Tiredness. That's all I've got to look forward to for the rest of my life. The grants have been granted and I haven't got one,' he proclaimed, bitterly. His eyelids drooped shut. To the concern of the two women, who were watching with polite attention, an extraordinary force of gravity seemed to pull McGregor's features earthwards. He forced his mouth open, baring his teeth in a fixed death's head grin. His fists were clenched. He remained like that for several moments in an epic struggle against invading tiredness. Then his face relaxed and his eyes shot open:

'A hundred pipers an a' an a',' he sang, enticingly, with the faintest of threats. The bus rounded a corner and the tobacco tin dropped from his knee to the floor. He regarded it with awe:

'Isn't it a wonderful thing,' he said, 'that the floor exists to stop things falling through the air?' He pocketed the tin and staggered to his feet. Eyes shut, he put both hands to his head. The mud in his hair gave it the texture of bark. McGregor enjoyed, for at least a minute, the knowledge that he had turned into a tree. He had the distinct sensation that his feet were putting down roots into the floor of the bus; his head sprouting branches that were about to push their way through the roof, each branch adorned with tingling, green buds. He shook his head and opened his eyes. The passengers sat dully before him. He regarded them with disdain and announced in the grand manner of an actor:

'I am leaving this travelling hearse!'

He made his way to the head of the stairs and turned once more, with a theatrical flourish, to address his reluctant audience:

'I hope your legs turn to gristle and chickens eat them!'

They heard his boots clattering, too fast, down the steps. The bus stopped. The word 'WANKERS' drifted up to them. Nobody moved. The passengers remained pinned to their seats by this new definition of themselves as the bus drew away.

In the underground station, the driver of the tube train leaned from his window and glared at McGregor with such malevolence, such implacable hatred written on his swarthy features, that McGregor was brought to a halt on the empty platform. The doors shut in McGregor's face. The driver continued to stare. The train remained stationary. McGregor launched into a sweet, tuneful whistle. Without warning, the driver turned and pressed a button. The doors hissed open. Within minutes of boarding the train, McGregor slept a profound and dreamless sleep, his legs stretched out across the gap between the seats.

In this way, McGregor was borne, deep in the intestinal passages of the earth, across London. Through the black tunnels, under the river, he was carried along, first in one direction and then another. Overhead, the mammoth city, with its millions of citizens in their neon-lit offices, went about its business. And not a solitary soul was aware that far beneath the ground underfoot, McGregor was voyaging.

McGregor opened his eyes. The train had stopped. The doors stood open. He got off without knowing which station he was in. The platform was deserted. The air was warm. A numbness in his feet made him unsure that they were touching the ground and gave him the feeling of floating through the yellow-lit passages and hallways. For all he knew, he had slept for three days and three nights. Under one arch, a black dog that had strayed into the underground blocked his way, bristling and barking. McGregor stopped and whistled at it. The dog lost interest and padded away, sniffing at the grimy, cream-tiled walls.

And then a wondrous sight met McGregor's eyes.

Where the tunnel opened out onto the flat area below the escalators, a black woman, in her forties, was dancing vigorously on the concourse under the high, domed ceiling. All on her own, she boogied and partied to strains of music that filtered down from the station entrance, a beatific smile on her face. In one hand she held a can of lager, taking swigs from it as her hips swung from side to side. Some other black commuters passed by, giving her a wide berth. McGregor watched, enchanted, as if all his travels had been expressly to bring him to this one point at this particular moment. One side of her coat hung down lower than the other and she'd hitched up her skirt into her belt. She finished the lager and threw down the can. It skittered over the floor with an echoing rattle close to where a uniformed transport guard was sweeping. Then she bebopped over to a pile of carrier-bags, dumped where the curved wall reached the ground and rummaged for some more beer. The side of her shoe was split open by the big-toe joint:

'Lard,' she said. 'Look how me shoe is poppin' offa me foot.' She opened the can, took a gulp and jived her way back to the centre of the hall. McGregor looked on appreciatively. Then she spotted him. Her eyes gleamed with pleasure:

'Come daalin'.' She addressed him with carefree boldness. 'Dance wid me, nuh.'

McGregor approached bashfully:

'Och. I canna dance,' he said.

'Everybody can dance,' she insisted and continued to shimmy round the hall. Suddenly, McGregor joined her, leaping into the air and executing a wild, jerky Highland fling accompanied by a joyous, warlike scream. The woman shook with laughter.

'You're beautiful,' said McGregor.

'Yuh lie,' she screeched with laughter again and stopped to catch her breath. 'It still snowin' up there?' she asked.

'I dunno,' said McGregor.

'Lemme tell you sometin'.' She beckoned him closer. 'I was up there and a cold wind from Russia came an' fasten in me back. That damn wind bit me like a snake. So I come down here.'

'And let me tell you something, lady,' said McGregor. 'You are the first person I have seen all day with a big smile on their face. And I love you for it.'

They regarded each other with mutual approval.

'Yuh sweet, man. Yuh come to carry me way wid you?' she teased. 'First yuh must gimme a kiss. Come nuh, man. Yuh gwaan kiss me or what?' she said boldly.

'Lady. You are the first real bit of humanity I've come across today, the first person with a wee bit of optimism and I'd love to kiss you.' She was close to him. Her breath smelled sweet and sharp like olives. He glanced round. The station had filled up with black people. He felt a little unsure of himself:

'Wait a minute. Wait a minute, lady.' He approached the guard who was still sweeping:

'Excuse me, sir. Excuse me – er this lady would like me to give her a kiss. Would that cause any bother at all?'

The guard stopped sweeping and surveyed the concourse. Three youths were lounging against the wall opposite. He scratched his head:

'Well, it just could do. A lot of these youts still hot-headed after the riots, you know. Them could jus' get hold of the wrong end of the stick, if you know what I mean. Them could jus' think "Here is another white man who think he own a black woman like all through history".' The guard touched McGregor kindly on the arm. 'I tell you what I suggest. You go on ahead up the stairs and let the lady follow you. Then we don' have no trouble. You can go for a nice drink together somewhere and see how you get on?' He winked. 'Lemme go tell her.'

He walked over to the woman who was fumbling in her plastic bag. He spoke to her for a few moments and then came back:

'You jus' go on up de stairs like I said. Don' even look back. Let she jus' pick up she bags and follow you.'

McGregor hesitated but the woman was smiling and blowing kisses at him:

'Right y'are then,' he said.

'Go on up. She will follow you. OK man?' The guard slapped him on the arm amicably.

McGregor did as he was asked. But he was hurt. Some poison had entered him. What the guard had said about history and white men went round in his head. He held onto the rail and the escalator carried him smoothly upwards. Half way up, he turned to check that she was following. Her eyes, blank with disappointment, were fixed on him and she was walking slowly backward away from him through the arched hallway, carrier-bags on each arm like white water-wings. He watched her disappearing as if she were being drawn back into the dark tunnel. Trying to get back down he slipped, cursed, stumbled and clung onto the rail. The escalator bore him steadily up towards the curtain of snow that hung in the station entrance. Something was happening to him that he did not recognise. A hot substance, like lava, crawled slowly down his cheeks.

Later that night, the police arrested a man in Camberwell. He was smashing shop windows, one after the other with a scaffolding spanner. As the glass exploded in each one, he yelled:

'I want you to know that I never owned a fucking slave in my life. Never.'

THE TRUTH IS
IN THE CLOTHES

Later, much later, I came to the conclusion that she was a manipulator, this black woman from Soweto; powerful certainly, a shrewd entrepreneur and a hugely talented designer, but, finally, without those powers of sorcery that I initially attributed to her. The gifts of the genuine shaman overlap in places with the psychological wizardry of the charlatan. After a lapse of time, I became convinced that her powers were more akin to those of the confidence trickster.

This is the story.

Late one night, there was a knock on my door. Zephra, my singer friend from Trinidad, stood on the doorstep with a small group of people. She was radiant, bubbling with that energy performers get after a show. Whether it was the light falling on her from the doorway or the brightness of the outfit she wore, I couldn't tell, but she eclipsed the others:

'Hi. Sorry to call so late.' Her eyes shone with exuberance. 'This is Kalimbo, a band from South Africa I've just been working with.' Two shortish men, one with a pork-pie hat, the other bare headed, stepped shyly over the threshold. Behind them entered a tall woman with a headwrap.

'Come in. Come in.' The front room had that air of peaceful expectancy that rooms unaccountably acquire after being tidied. 'I've only got rum in the house. Will that do everybody?' The woman asked for fruit juice.

Zephra trailed after me into the kitchen, chatting while I fixed rum drinks with ice, freshly squeezed limes and Cassis:

'Old Oak rum!' she squealed. 'I ain' seen that since I was home.'

It was good to see her so happy, Zephra, with her tremulous spirit and history of breakdowns. She was still thin, her eyes enormous in a gaunt, brown face. I ignored the remnants of a black eye, a tiny, upturned crescent of crimson under her right eye.

'What are you wearing?' I asked. 'It looks wonderful.'

Under the bright kitchen lights, she held up her arms to show off the outfit. Shocking pink cotton cloth with great, batwing sleeves hung down to her mid-calves. Printed in black on the cloth were African heads and the occasional brilliant green banana tree set against a hot orange sun. Her hat was pill-box shaped, the same bright pink, edged with black and with two stiffened, black, batwing shapes on either side.

'Isn't it beautiful?' she said. 'I tell you, girl, when I step out on that stage tonight, these clothes uplifted my spirit. My songs just took off like a flight of birds. You must check out this band. You will love their music. I know it.'

We took the drinks back into the front room. It was darker in there, lit only by a table-lamp. The men were seated in a corner, talking quietly. The woman stood in the centre of the room.

'This is Maisie.' Zephra introduced her.

'I am pleased to meet you.' The voice was low and sweet as an underground river. She was a broad but lean-faced African woman with thin lips, her complexion charcoal black with patches of bronze on the cheekbones. I guessed she was about forty, tall and rangy. The light raincoat she held bunched round her was the colour of earth but in no way drab. Round her head, she had twisted, carelessly but with immense style, a rough piece of maroon cloth patterned with a diagram of white drumsticks.

Zephra plumped herself down on the sofa, took a packet of ganga from her bag and began to build a spliff. Maisie sat down in the armchair next to the four-foot-high weeping-fig plant. I sat on the floor.

'Are you all from Soweto?' I asked.

'Yes,' the man with the pork-pie hat and fat, brown eyelids

replied. 'We are from the Naledi township.' The men exchanged words in their own language and laughed.

'They are telling you that I am from the Rockville area. One of the electrified areas,' said Maisie.

'It was Maisie who made me these clothes,' chimed in Zephra. 'I needed something for the gig tonight and she ran this up for me in an hour!'

'That is what I do.' Maisie spoke with soft intimacy. 'I am a designer of clothes. I make the clothes for the band. In Africa I make clothes for many artists. Musicians come from far seeking my clothes. They like to be photographed in them for the front of their albums. They know my clothes can make them successful. They can make people into stars. They can make people live long. My clothes can kill people. My clothes can heal people. I tell you, the truth is in the clothes.'

She leaned towards me. Her eyes were a lighter brown than most African eyes. The ear-rings dangling from her ears were long, silver ones with tiny chains hanging from the bottom:

'When I make clothes for performing artists,' she continued, 'other artists become jealous. Competitive. They consult a witch-doctor for potions and herbs to take away the magic from my clothes. Powerful African mixtures,' she muttered as though I would not understand. 'When performers do that – try to bewitch another performer who is wearing my clothes – then I get sick, because they are trying to kill me at home. Twice I have been in the hospital vomiting blood. I carry on because I am guided. I see something about the person and I am guided to make the clothes. Are you a journalist?' she asked, unexpectedly. She must have seen the typewriter and clutter of papers on the table. 'I want you to write something about me.'

'I don't write that sort of thing. I write stories,' I apologised. 'I might write a story about you, about someone who makes clothes that can kill or heal people. That would make a good story.'

'You must do that,' she said.

Zephra rifled through the cassette tapes. She dug out some Cuban salsa music and slapped it in the machine. Then she began to dance. The men talked between themselves in location language.

'I like you,' said Maisie. 'I will make something for you. A beautiful jacket.' I was flattered as if someone had offered to paint my portrait. Immediately, I wanted that jacket more than anything in the world.

'I will pay you, of course,' I said. Payment did not seem enough. 'But I will also write the story about you. I will make a story for you in exchange for the jacket.'

The light from the table-lamp shone up through the weeping-fig and threw dappled shadows of leaves onto the ceiling over her head. Suddenly, I saw her quite clearly sitting on a wooden bench in Africa. She was leaning forward under the shade of a great, spreading tree. Behind her, on the other side of a chicken-wire fence, sprawled an estate of yellow, matchbox housing. I smelled a burning smell. Creosote or burning rubber. In her left hand she held a piece of corn. Fine, silky brown hair sprouted from the top. Maisie. The name itself reminded me of corn and fertility; roots growing in the earth that can be ground and made into nourishment. Maisie. A fermenting, bubbling name, golden like mead. Mealie meal. Finely ground maize. Maisie.

'I want to make a film.' She was back sitting in the chair. 'Can you help me to do that?' she asked, abruptly.

'I don't think so,' I said. 'Where? Here or in Africa?'

'Anywhere. I travel extensively.' She paused, then added, 'The United States.'

'I'll try and think of someone who could help you. How are things in Soweto?' I enquired, respectfully sympathetic.

'I am not an oppressed woman,' she snapped. 'And my people are not oppressed.'

Conversation in the room had ceased. The Cubans shouted gaily from the machine. My little black cat, Basil, strolled in, tail on high and rubbed himself around her legs.

Zephra switched off the cassette player:

'We have to go now,' she announced. 'Some people are expecting us.'

I knew if I lost track of them I would lose my jacket:

'Where can I find you all?'

'I've got to go to Manchester tomorrow,' said Zephra. 'The

band will be playing at the Club Sozo in the Seven Sisters Road.
Go down there tomorrow night.'

'Will you be there?' I asked Maisie.

'Yes. I will be there,' she said.

We said our goodbyes. I showed them to the door.

Next evening I squeezed into the back of the Club Sozo. It was
packed. Squinting in the dark, I tried reading the promo leaflet:
'Kalimbo style – spirit of ancestors. Benda region. Benda
people. Used by many tribes. Crossing of traditional with
popular music of townships.'

One of the men on stage had not been at my flat the night
before, a thin man. The skin head of his drum was anchored by
strings to the pegs round the outside. The rhythms vibrated
through the crowd. But it was not his playing that attracted my
attention. It was what he wore. He wore a most extraordinary
suit, the shape of Africa. The suit was made of dark green cotton
with fiery orange and yellow markings. The pants were baggy.
The right sleeve made up the enormous bulge of the West Coast.
The left sleeve cut away sharply, following the outline of the
coast of Ethiopia, dipping up to Somaliland and the Horn of
Africa. Stitched onto the front was a pocket, also shaped like
Africa, in black with the same hectic markings. The southern
part of the continent fell just below his knees. As he slapped the
drum, fire crackled all over the cloth. I looked for Maisie in the
audience. There was no sign of her.

The cramped dressing-room smelled of stale beer. Some kind of
ruck was going on. The promoter, a thin-faced Englishman, was
angry. The night before, the drummer had been drunk, too
paralytic to perform. Now the promoter would not give them
their full fee. Maisie sat sulking in a corner. The men were
arguing but I could see they were subdued, depressed. The
guitarist smiled a hello at me with sad eyes:

'We are homesick,' he said. 'The tour has been a long one.'

I went over and crouched at Maisie's feet in the small
space:

'When can I come and see you about my jacket?'

'I don't know,' she said, then changed her mind. 'Tomorrow.
Give me a pen and paper. I will write down the address where I

will be in the morning.' She wrote down an address somewhere in Camberwell.

The address was difficult to find, nowhere near an underground station. The August morning was dull and overcast. I had to walk up the drives of several of the large Victorian houses because the numbers were either missing or not clear. When finally I found it, the front door was open. I walked in. The house was in the process of being renovated into flats, floor-boards bare, wires sticking out from wall sockets. I called her name:

'Maisie.' There was no reply. I walked up the stairs.

She was already at work on the third floor. The room stank of hot wax and vegetable oil. A welter of mainly brownish cloth festooned the place, draped over sofa, floor and chairs. Patches of the green cloth worn by the drummer lay here and there, jumbled with other fragments and scraps of material. Strung across the windows were swatches of cloth, the colour of caramel rivers. Beside an ancient, two-ring burner stood Maisie, stirring vigorously the wax in a rusty tin can. She wore a shift of the softest brushed cotton thinly striped in grey and pink, Arab style, and a headwrap of the same stuff.

'Come in and sit down.'

I found a stool and squatted on it. She worked as she talked.

'You see how fast I work? When I was in America I made one thousand tie and dye pieces in five days, each one a different colour, a different design. They refused to believe I had done it.' She sounded bitter. 'They tried to cheat me. They said I only made seven hundred. I refused the money they were offering because it was less than what I had been promised. I do not make the clothes for money. Money is drawn to me but I do not make the clothes because of money. God speaks to me. I am guided by him. I follow whatever he says. In America they said I was a witch.'

Metal buckets of dye gleamed dully on the floor, indigo, dark green, vermilion. As she spoke she dipped cloth, intricately tied with string, into one or another bucket. The liquid never spilled. Then she started to paint the hot wax onto the cotton in strong, bold patterns. She would crack the wax on other pieces of cloth, where it had dried, re-dip the cloth and force the new colour into the fissures and creases she formed constantly with her hands.

'How did you discover you had this gift?' I was impressed.

'Always, always I loved clothes. From when I was tiny. If my mother wanted to punish me she would forbid me to wear my favourite clothes. My mother was an Anglican. My father a Methodist. I ran from my mother and went to my father's church. That is where I heard the story of the coat of many colours. I knew I could make one. Wherever I go I borrow the equipment I need to make clothes. I cannot stop.'

I watched her twist the cloth into special folds.

'When I was little I would put pebbles and stones, even bricks, into the cloth to make the shapes I needed. I stitched with raffia. I had to use tamarind water and indigo for dye. Now I use cold water dyes, but I use them hot. I use caustic soda to fix the colours and sodium sulphate to make the white more brilliant. God has helped me. I have three factories where people sew for me. I have two shops, one in the airport at Bophuthatswanaland. You must help me find an outlet in England.'

She strung up the cloth to dry. Curiously, no drips fell from it. She took up a length of material and began to cut. She cut boldly, sleeves and body of the wrap from a single piece of cloth. I tried to bring the conversation round to my jacket:

'Do you need to take my measurements for the jacket?'

'No. I have looked at you. That is enough.'

I tried to resist asking but couldn't:

'What will it be like?'

'I shall make you a jacket of royal blue. I like working with royal blue. I shall line it with red. And there will be things on it. Things that are for you especially.'

Excitement ground the pit of my stomach. Something else I wanted to know:

'How is it you say your clothes can kill people?'

'Whatever is done in the clothes affects the man himself. That is not my responsibility. God tells me what to do. The clothes can kill. The clothes can heal. That is God's will, not mine.'

In the corner on a table rested an old treadle sewing-machine. She seated herself at it:

'One time when I could not find what it was I wanted to wear,

I took down the curtains in my house and quickly made them into a new outfit.' She laughed.

I took fifty pounds from my purse:

'Is fifty pounds enough for the jacket?'

She answered through the whirr of the machine:

'That is enough. Put it on the table. I do not pursue money but I do not like to be cheated. I do not make clothes for the money.'

I could hardly believe that. Three factories? Two shops? Business trips all over the world?

'I am leaving for Zimbabwe the day after tomorrow,' she said. 'When I am gone I want you to go to Harrods and tell them about my clothes.'

'I'll try,' I said, doubtfully. 'Will you have time to make my jacket?'

'Write your name and address down on a piece of paper and leave it with me. The jacket will come to you.'

I did as she asked.

'Thank you very much, Maisie.' I got up to leave. She got up too. 'Will you be coming back to England?'

'January. I will come back in January. Goodbye. Don't forget you must write a nice story about me.'

I turned back in the doorway to wave goodbye. She stood facing me, her back to the window. Everywhere in the room the cloth had formed itself into a miniature landscape around her. A female Ozymandias, she bestrode the desert. Behind her were steep escarpments, grooved cliffs of brown sandstone. Tiny mountain ranges obscured her feet. In front of me stretched a panorama of dried-out river beds, dizzying whorls of sand, hillocks and dunes patched with green oases. All this I saw with the scale and clarity of detail as though from an ascending aeroplane. It lasted for a split second. Then the room returned to normal. I left, again the smell of burning rubber in my nostrils.

Four days later the jacket arrived, delivered by hand, in a brown paper parcel tied with string. I unpacked it. In length the garment was half way between a coat and a jacket, reaching to mid-thigh. It was cut, all in one, with wide sleeves like a kaftan. Outside, as she had promised, the colour was a magnificent royal blue. The lining was deep red. Round about the hem there alternated a golden bell and a pomegranate, the same around the hem of the sleeves. Strikingly printed all over the blue exterior and the red lining were black shapes. I examined them more closely. They were scarabs, the sacred beetle of ancient Egypt.

I went straight to the mirror to try it on. It fitted perfectly but somehow I was disappointed. It made me look pale and wasted. Several times over the next few months, I tried it on. The result was always the same. Either I looked ill or, when it did suit me, I could find nothing to wear with it. In the end I left it hanging in the cupboard.

January came and went. No sign of Maisie. Shortly after she left I tried to write a story about her but nothing came. I decided that it was my own suggestibility that had endowed her with supernatural powers and I felt foolish.

I forgot about her. A year later I was working on a collection of short stories. I needed three more. I remember that it was a Wednesday evening and I was sitting, browsing through old notebooks searching for ideas. I found a few notes on Maisie. Perhaps I could knock them into a story. I wrote the first unflattering paragraph, stating that she was no more than a con-woman. As I completed it, the telephone rang. I heard the blip and squeak of a long-distance call, then the voice, quite clear:

'Hello. This is Julia.' I tried to think who it might be.

'Julia Legwabe,' the voice said as if I should know it.

'Hi,' I bluffed. 'Where are you?'

'Bophuthatswanaland,' came the reply. 'Maisie says you must meet her at the airport on Friday.'

I glanced guiltily over at the page sticking out of the typewriter:

'I'm afraid I can't. I'm working on Friday.' I lied.

'All right. Thank you very much. I will tell her. Goodbye.' The receiver at the other end clicked down.

Unnerved by the timing of the call, I felt that she was heading over here to stop me writing the truth about her. I decided to go ahead and worked late that night and all through the next day. In the evening the telephone rang. This time it was her:

'Hello. This is Maisie,' said the husky voice, intimate even at a distance of thousands of miles.

'Hello,' I said with false delight. 'Where are you?'

'Mafeking,' she said. I had a picture of her flitting around the southern part of Africa, one minute in Bophuthatswanaland, the next in Mafeking.

'I am coming to London on Sunday. I want to stay with you.'

'Oh no. What a shame. I won't be in London. I'm working out of town.' I hoped she mistook my hesitation for the normal time-lag of a long-distance call.

'That is a pity because I am having a show. I wanted you to see it.'

'Maybe I can get back for a bit. Where is it?'

'The South African Embassy.'

I was shocked.

'I can't go in there,' I said. 'There's a cultural boycott. There's a picket outside. There's a continuous twenty-four-hour demonstration in front of the Embassy.'

'I know.' She chuckled. 'You should come with me. You might learn something.'

'How long will you be in London?'

'Just for the show on Monday. Then I go to Belgium and Austria.'

'Oh, I'm sorry. It looks as though I will miss you.' I paused. 'I haven't written that story about you yet.'

It was not a lie. It was not the truth.

'A lot of people want to write about me. You must write a nice story about me.'

'OK. Goodbye, Maisie.' I hung up.

I returned to the typewriter. So far what I had written was a condemnation of her as a fraud, a sell-out, a reactionary, a collaborator. Now I decided I would not write about her at all. I would scrap the whole idea. I took the pages and chucked them in the bin.

I'd taken the jacket out and laid it open on the sofa to remind me of the style and feel of her work, hoping it would lead me into the story. I stared at it. The black scarab shapes on the scarlet lining appeared to shift. I blinked to clear my eyes. The second time I looked they shifted more violently. That happens sometimes with the juxtaposition of red and black. It is an optical illusion, something to do with the structure of the cells at the back of the retina. I shut my eyes for a full minute. When I looked again, both the blue exterior of the jacket and the red lining were completely plain. There was nothing on them at all. Slowly, I raised my eyes. The black shapes were all over the wall and half-way across the ceiling. I looked away and looked back. They were still there.

The cat started to use the leg of the table as a scratching post. I pushed him down. Immediately, he levitated, rotating upright, his four legs outspread. With a sudden change of speed and direction, he hurled himself against the back wall and buried himself in the plaster causing thin, jagged cracks. I went over for a closer inspection. There was, where he had sunk in, a wide, cork plug in the wall, the sort of stopper you see in glass jars in fashionable kitchens. I manoeuvred it out. Through the hole in the wall I could see dusty catacombs. I was able to hear footsteps in there, but I saw nobody. I pulled away enough bits of plaster and masonry to be able to squeeze through.

The yellow porous rock crumbled a little under my touch. Rough walls were pitted with holes containing grains of sand. Light came from somewhere but I couldn't discover the source. There was no trace of damp and the air was warm. To my left, in a hollowed-out cave, a man lay groaning on the ground, his shirt wrapped tightly round him. I approached. Over his head some letters were scratched in the wall. The letters were all constructed of straight lines. As I studied them they lit up as if someone had shone a torch from behind me. I read:

H . . . E . . . R . . . A . . . K . . . L . . . The last letters were indecipherable.

I did not go too close to the man because I knew his shirt was poisoned.

I passed through the honeycombed passages and came to the bottom of a staircase. It was familiar. I recognised it as the staircase of a London house where I had lived some years earlier in a flat on the top floor. I climbed the stairs. The house appeared to be unoccupied. Where there had been carpeting on the stairs, the boards were bare and dusty. I held onto the wooden banister and went up to the top. The flat was empty, the windows dirty, and my shoes made tapping noises on the floorboards. I opened the door to what used to be the living room.

To my surprise I found myself at the back of an evangelical church hall. A phalanx of wooden chairs waited for a congregation. The only occupants were two women seated some way apart, one in a drab maroon coat, the other in dull green. A flush of embarrassment came over me. What would my friends think if they discovered I had a functioning church in my front room? There was no altar, just a high pulpit set in front of the chairs. An Anglican vicar entered from the back and made his way down the left-hand aisle to the pulpit. His white surplice hung limply over the black gown. Steel grey streaked the hair on the back of his head. He mounted the pulpit:

'Today's sermon is taken from two readings of the Old Testament: the first from Exodus, Chapter 39, verses 24–26 and the second from Ecclesiastes, Chapter 3, verses 1–3.'

The voice was weary:

' "*And they made upon the hems of the robe, pomegranates of blue and purple, and scarlet, and twined linen.*

And they made bells of pure gold and put the bells between the pomegranates upon the hem of the robe, round about between the pomegranates;

A bell and a pomegranate, a bell and a pomegranate round about the hem of the robe." '

The church smelled musty. He continued with monotonous intonation:

' "*To everything there is a season, and a time to every purpose under the heaven:*

A time to be born and a time to die; a time to plant and a time to pluck up that which is planted;

A time to kill and a time to heal . . ." '

I slipped out through the side door into the sunshine.

The grass beneath my feet was dry and brown, the heat overpowering. Dolores was hanging out clothes on the line strung between the mango tree and Mr Elliot's house. Water glistened on her brown hands. As she reached for the pegs her dress rode up round her strong thighs. I couldn't believe that I had lived in my ground floor London flat for five years without ever realising that Jamaica was just on the other side of my back wall. Relief flooded me. Now I would be able to return whenever I wanted, by going through the hole in the wall:

'Hi there, Dolores.'

She turned, smiling:

'Hi there to you too. 'Ave you seen Mr Elliot? 'Im say 'im a soon come but 'im don' reach yet.' She spoke in her slow, country accent.

'I ain' seen him.'

Every day Dolores walked three miles across Kingston to look after Mr Elliot's children while his wife was in America:

'Thirta dollars 'im say 'im woudda give me today. Thirta dollars.'

She sprinkled some Coldpower from a packet into a tin tub full of white washing. The clothes squeaked as she rubbed them. Another tub on the ground contained the clean water for rinsing. Heat prickled the back of my neck. A bird was cursing in the hedge.

'How are the children?' I knew that the father of her two children had deserted her for a rich man's daughter.

'They doin' fine. Is me mudda raise dem now. She don' barn dem but she do raise dem.'

'Do you ever hear from Fat-Boy?'

'Not one word. Not one dollar. But ah washin' this for 'im now.' She held up a long, dazzling white robe. The brilliance of the white hurt my eyes. It reminded me of the garb worn for the pocomania ritual.

'I'm surprised you're doing anything for him,' I said.

She convulsed with laughter:

'It's the media,' she said. I must have looked confused. She laughed again, this time astonished at my lack of comprehension.

'You don' hunnerstan'? It's the MEEDEEA.' She doubled up, clutching the robe to her chest, creased with laughter.

I left her and went into the house. In Mr Elliot's bedroom lay the jumble and clutter of a man whose wife is away. The room was stuffy. I turned the handle of a door to the right of the bed. It opened onto a room which I recognised immediately as the place where I was supposed to be.

The ceiling was high. The walls were built of great, square, yellow stone slabs. The room was no bigger than a cell. I shut the door gently behind me. Everything was peaceful. The only furniture was a small wooden table with a wooden chair set by it. The wood was rough and white and reminded me of the wooden draining-board we had at home which my mother used to scrub with parazone. On the table stood a typewriter. Sunlight fell on it from a window that was no more than a slit in the enormously thick walls. Placed next to the typewriter was an opened packet of plain foolscap paper.

I took out a sheet of paper and inserted it in the typewriter. I barely needed to touch the keys. The typewriter wrote of its own accord:

THE TRUTH IS IN THE CLOTHES

YOU LEFT THE DOOR OPEN

Some events defy scrutiny. Like electrons in a bubble-chamber, the act of looking at them disturbs them. All that can be seen are traces of recent passage, tracks left behind. The electron itself remains unseen, its form only to be guessed at, a ghost in the atom.

The attack – and it was a violent one, a murderous one, at night, as I lay sleeping – was just such an event. Under close examination, the meaning of it began to dance. There were traces, both before and after, that served as clues; synchronicities, unaccountable coincidences, signs even, as well as solid facts and evidence. But, at the heart of the matter lay impenetrable ambiguity, like the infuriating Necker cube – a cube drawn in such a way that one minute it appears solid and facing in one direction and then, through an involuntary shift in the mechanism of the eye, it appears to be hollow and facing the other way.

The paradigm, the lens through which something is viewed, determines what is seen. Psychologists, with their particular conceptual spectacles, saw the attack as the work of a paranoid schizophrenic. Sociologists would doubtless have some other explanation for the epidemic of stranglings and rapes that plagued London throughout the long, hot summer of that year. Theories that include the idea of a demon are, of course, out of the question in this day and age. Demons have lost their footing on the hierarchy of scientific disciplines. The police lay yet another template on events. Their gaze rests only on the physical, forensic evidence and facts:

'Did you notice anyone suspicious hanging around the area before you were attacked?' A buxom policewoman in a spotlessly white blouse and neat skirt was taking down my statement.

'Yes, I did. A few days earlier I saw a man sitting on the low wall outside one of the houses a few doors down the street.'

'What did this man look like?' she asked.

'He looked as though he had the soul of a wolf,' I replied.

The policewoman did not write this down. Her pen remained poised over the sheaf of statement papers. It was not the sort of fact the police wish to accumulate:

'Did you notice what he was wearing?' she asked.

I tried to remember the physical details. It had been a warm day, yet he had been wearing a jacket, blue or grey, I think. I passed him, sitting on the wall, as I returned home from the shops; a man in his late thirties, with a broad forehead and fairish hair receding at the temples, lean in build. As I approached him, the hairs on the back of my hands prickled and rose. There seemed to be some sort of aura around him like an electro-magnetic force-field. He stared at me and through me and past me. What struck me was that he looked more utterly alone than anyone I have ever seen. Schoolchildren were tumbling out of the gates of the school across the road. For a moment I felt a brief, inexplicable concern for their safety, but I gave him no more than a glance as I returned home. A couple of hours later, I went out again. The man was still sitting there.

I am a cabaret artist. I specialise in impersonations. Not for me the grand, plush venues of London, I work in the tiny clubs, the underground cellars hung with black drapes where the audiences are impecunious and raucous. On this circuit, there is usually one cramped room put aside as a dressing room. Jugglers, comics, fire-eaters and musicians vie for space amid dirty tables, empty beer cans and plastic cups sprouting cigarette ends hastily doused as some performer hears his name being announced by the compère on stage. A few months before the main events of this story took place – the attack occurred in the summer and I suppose the idea first came to me in February – I was becoming bored with my act and I conceived the idea of doing some male impersonation. One night, alone at home, I found myself in the bathroom looking in the cabinet mirror. I took a black eyebrow pencil from my make-up bag and drew a moustache on my upper lip. It was too thick. I made it thinner. Then I took some hair gel from the shelf and smarmed my hair back off my face. I spent an inordinate amount of time combing my hair. I thickened my eyebrows and looked at the face in the mirror. It grinned. It was the face of a small-time crook, a petty thief. I settled on a name for him – Charlie. The next day, I went to the market to find Charlie some clothes. A cold drizzle fell on the stalls of second-hand clothes and cheap jewellery. I selected the following items for him:

A black nylon roll-neck sweater, the type worn by spivs.
A calf-length camel-hair coat.
Some flashy, fake gold rings and a neck-chain.
A pork-pie hat, brown with a feather in it.
Hush-puppy shoes, soft and noiseless.
Second-hand grey trousers with a sharp crease.

That evening, Charlie regarded me confidently from the full-length mirror in my bedroom. I decided to take him out in the street. The night was damp and freezing cold. I hate the cold. Charlie seemed to love it. He had not spoken much but when he had it was with a northern accent. One odd thing I noticed. Normally, I am short-sighted, but that evening I could see far, way down the street. Outside, standing on the pavement, I knew immediately that Charlie was vicious and predatory. All he wanted to do was to wait in shop doorways and pounce on passers-by. I didn't let him, of course. But before I could stop him, he had taken my car keys and let himself into my car. He drove too fast, cursing and swearing at any delay, pushing the nose of the car right up against the bumpers of other, slower cars in front. He wanted to hurt people. There was a certain thrill to his viciousness. I took him home. I was exhausted. He wasn't. I undressed and went to bed.

A short while later, I took him on stage for the first time. It was a mistake. He had not the least intention of amusing the audience.

He wanted to frighten them. He said horrible things. Quickly, I took Charlie home and put him away in the cupboard.

'What happened to that character you were creating?' a friend enquired of me, a week or so after his debut.

'Oh, he was too violent and dangerous,' I giggled. 'He had to be locked up in a mental hospital.'

Around the time I discovered Charlie, a man was, in fact, released from one of the big hospitals for the criminally insane in the north of England. Later, he was to weep, his head on the table in the police interview room, saying that the hospital was the only place where he had ever been happy. Outside, apparently, a voice kept getting into his head telling him to do certain things. He consistently denied the attack. 'It wasn't me,' he repeated again and again. 'It wasn't me.' In some ways, he may have been right.

In May, I read in the local newspaper that a woman who lived nearby had been savagely attacked and raped by a man who was skilful and cunning enough to leave not a fingerprint or trace of himself behind. I soon forgot about it.

A sizzling summer arrived. A Jamaican friend of mine came to stay while she finalised the last details of the publication of her book. On the day she was to leave, we were sitting with friends who had come to say good-bye. The flat was a welter of half-packed suitcases, pages of manuscript, scattered books and possible designs for her book cover.

'I don't like any of these designs for the book jacket,' she grumbled. 'I won't have them on the front of my book.' She shoved some clothes into a bag and turned to one of the other girls:

'Mary, your designs are better than these. Go and do some sketches for me, quick. Take them down to the publishers on Monday and send me copies to Jamaica. I must have something with more of a Caribbean feel to it.'

Mary was on her knees studying the front covers of several books laid out on the floor. She looked up at the bookshelf and saw, resting there, a painting I had brought back with me from Haiti. Still unframed, it leant against the wall. It is a smallish painting, executed in the most brilliant colours. A leopard, one of the sacred animals of Haiti, sits under a tree in the forest. From the branches of the tree hang large, round fruits, purple, brown and scarlet sliced with yellow. The great cat, black with no markings, gazes out from thick, green foliage. His eyes are bright, lucent and alert. They appear to follow you round the room as you move.

'Let me borrow that painting,' said Mary. 'The colours have the right feel.' I did not want her to borrow the painting. It is my favourite. She will spoil it, I thought, drop coffee on it, sit on it and tear the canvas. I tried to invent an excuse as to why she could not take it:

'Don't take that painting. It protects my house,' I mumbled, feebly. But she took it anyway, promising to bring it back the next day. And that night, without its protection, I was attacked.

In the afternoon, after I had driven my friend to the airport and tidied the flat a little, I sat at the table in the front room trying to complete some work. Once, I looked up and a figure darted behind some bushes that grow by the railings in the front garden. I did not see the face. I thought no more of it. That evening, I visited friends. It must have been about one o'clock in the morning when I returned home. I remember hearing the sound of my heels clicking in the empty street as I ran from my car to the flat. It is always a disturbing sound, running footsteps at night, even if they are your own. The sound of a victim. Inside the flat, I felt safe. It was peaceful and warm. I put my bag and keys on the trunk by the front door and wandered into the large back bedroom. There, I undressed and hung my clothes in the walk-in wardrobe. Naked, I strolled into the bathroom, washed and cleaned my teeth. For some reason, I decided to sleep in the small bedroom that night. It is a tiny room. In the corner opposite the door is a single divan bed. Next to the bed is a small cupboard with a portable television set on it and a radio clock. Apart from that, there is room only for an upright bamboo chair. Two uncurtained windows are set deep in the thick, outside walls of the house. I got into bed and switched on the television. For a while, I read by the light of the television. No other lights in the flat were on. After a bit, I reached over, switched off the television and went to sleep.

What woke me I do not know. I lifted my head from the pillow to see, dimly, a figure in the doorway about four feet away from me. The room was very dark. The figure recoiled for an instant. Then it attacked. I had the impression of something erupting violently from beneath the floorboards at the side of the bed. At the same time, a rough, gloved hand was pushing into and against my mouth, forcing my head down in the pillows. This is real, I thought, this is real. I struggled to breathe and I must have been trying to scream because the voice in my ear was saying:

'Shut up! Shut up! I've got a knife. I've got a knife.'

The voice was coarse and rough as goatskin. Scarcely able to breathe, I turned my head this way and that to get air. The whole weight of his body bore down on me. The rough, woollen-gloved hand clamped like a vice over my mouth was tearing the skin off my face as I twisted my head, trying to get away. I was suffocating. Sound that had its origin in my stomach was issuing out of my mouth, a roaring, black vomit of sound. He was still growling:

'Shut up! Shut up! Don't move! Don't move!'

The fight became a grim battle. Something was being pulled round my neck. Rope. As he tightened it, I put up my right hand and managed to insert my fingers under the rope and pull it away from my wind-pipe. I pulled and pulled. It came away in my hand and I held on to it tightly. Somehow, I contrived to swing my legs out of the bed. It was too dark to see anything clearly. He was standing over me. I lunged for his balls. We fought violently in the pitch-dark room. The television set crashed to the floor and then the radio clock went as well. The bamboo chair was smashed. I was pinioned back down on the bed, still struggling:

'I want to put a pillow-case over your head,' he grunted.

I bellowed: 'NOOOOOOOOOOOOO!'

The tidal wave of noise that came from me lifted me to my feet and him with me. He darted behind me and locked his left arm tightly round my neck. We were both out of breath. There we stood. I was captured. Naked and cunning as a wild animal, I trembled. I looked about, as far as the dim light would allow, for a weapon. Nothing in sight. I was filled with a sensation of extraordinary physical fitness and well-being. All I knew was that I had no intention of being quenched, snuffed out, extinguished, murdered and silenced. I had no intention of vacating my premises and leaving my empty body in the concrete gully beneath my window. Something diabolical had entered the flat. I would fight. But, he might be too strong in the end. Events seemed to have lifted themselves onto a plane where the struggle which took place felt like the ultimate, gargantuan struggle between good and evil. There was, as yet, no winner.

Suddenly, I punched out hard over my left shoulder. My fist smacked into his eye socket. I lashed out twice more. I tried to look round at his face but he jerked his head back so that I caught the merest glimpse of a high forehead, shining in the meagre light from the window, and a strand or two of fairish hair. I never saw his face. I jabbed my flat, stiffened fingers into his gullet and held them there, pushing hard. He countered by grabbing my hand and bending the fingers back violently. More fighting and we fell to the floor. It ended with my recapture. He sat with his back to the bedside cupboard, his left arm locked once more around my neck. I sat with my legs outstretched, his left leg curled about my waist. My back was to him. I saw the grubby trainer shoe on his foot. I was tired. I wanted to fall into a deep sleep.

'Don't move or I'll hurt you,' he kept saying.

In a mockery of snug intimacy, I sat nestled between the legs of the man whose face I had not seen. We stayed locked together like this for some considerable time, in fact, until the first birdsong at the break of dawn. The battleground changed. It became a battle of wills and of wits. For the first time, we conversed.

'Listen.' The voice was gruff and urgent. 'I want three things. I want money, food and a bath. I've been on the run for three days and I'm filthy. I'm filthy and I'm starving hungry.'

When he said he was filthy, I got the impression he was describing his inner self.

'Look,' he said, 'I've got to put a pillow-case over your head.'

'No,' I replied. 'That's too frightening.'

Now we were to bargain over every move, the advantage slipping from one to the other.

'All right, then. All right. I'm going to tie up your hands and feet. Give me the rope back.'

'No.' I still held tightly on to the thin piece of rope.

'I've got another piece here.' He reached in his pocket with his free hand and dangled a second piece in front of my face.

'I don't want you to tie me up. You might rape me.'

'If I was going to do that, I'd knock you spark out. If I was going to hurt you, I'd have done it by now. Give me my rope back.'

'No. I'm too scared.' My mind raced. I knew I had to keep him talking. 'Where are you on the run from, anyway?' I asked.

'I didn't escape from nick. The police were coming to pick me up and I went on the run from them.'

'My husband's on the run too,' I said, trying to make common ground between us.

'Well, I hope he doesn't end up in the same nick as me after all this.' There was a pause.

'He did diamond robberies,' I said.

'Is that where you got the money for the flat from?' I detected a strong, northern accent.

'Yes,' I said.

'Where is he now?' he asked, suspiciously.

'I dunno.' I tried making a bond between us. 'I'm on your side, you know. Let me go. I won't call the police. Most people I know are on the run, anyway.'

Playing for time, I embarked on a story of how a friend of mine escaped from jail. How she took a chance when one of the screws wasn't looking and ran off from the party working on the outside gardens. How she knocked on the door of a stranger's house and asked to use the telephone to call a taxi. My captor grunted to show that he was listening.

'Naturally, as she'd just done a bunk, she didn't have any money on her. So when the taxi came, she drove to a jeweller's, told the cabbie to stop for a minute, ran into the shop, sold the gold chain from round her neck and that's how she got the money to pay for the taxi.'

'Then what?' he asked.

'Then – and this is brilliant,' I continued, 'she went to a battered wives' hostel, told them she'd run away from a violent husband and they took her in. They hid her, helped her change her name by deed-poll and got her re-housed. Now she's living round the corner with her four kids.'

He gave his grunting laugh.

'So why don't you just go away,' I suggested quietly. 'I won't call the police. I don't like them any more than you do. How long do you want me to give you to get away?'

'Three weeks,' he replied. We both laughed.

'Now listen,' he said, 'I want you to put your hands together so I can tie you up.'

'No. That's too scary. You take what you want and I'll just sit here and I won't say anything.'

He became agitated.

'You won't,' he said. 'I don't trust you. I don't trust you. You'll do something. You'll do something.'

'I won't,' I said. But I knew I would, given a chance. And he knew it too.

'Are you a rapist or a burglar?' I asked.

'I'm a professional burglar. I'm a professional burglar.' He spoke with the insistence of a man trying to convince himself.

'Look,' he said. 'I'm not going to hurt you. It's you that's hurt me. I only attacked you once. You've attacked me twice. I'm still seeing stars from where you punched me.'

'Sorry,' I replied with false contrition. 'Anyway, I don't punch hard. I'm no Frank Bruno. I feel more like Barry McGuigan.' I had recently seen Barry McGuigan on television being carried, bloodstained and defeated, from the boxing ring.

The man laughed. I decided to play for sympathy.

'Ooh. I'm feeling sick,' I said. 'I think I'm going to faint.'

'Don't give me that shit,' he hissed and I stopped.

'Don't move,' he said, 'I'm going to roll myself a smoke.' He took his arm from my neck and began to feel for cigarette papers.

'Don't bother to roll one. There's a packet of mine on that little cupboard behind you. I want one too.' He felt around for them in the dark.

'Where?' he asked. 'I can't find them.'

'They must have fallen on the floor in the fight,' I replied.

He found them and lit one for me.

'What's your name?' he asked.

'Carole. What shall I call you?' I phrased the question in that way because I knew he wouldn't give me his real name. He hesitated for a minute and then answered:

'Charlie. Charlie Peace.'

It was not till days later that I discovered the true identity of Charlie Peace. The true historical identity that is – not the identity of the man who held me captive. Charlie Peace was a nineteenth-century murderer. He was born in Sheffield, son of a shoemaker. He was employed as a tinsmith and later as a workman at a rolling mill. Strangely enough, he also worked for a while as a cabaret artist. He appeared on stage in Worksop in 1853, a comic performance in which he impersonated the modern Paganini, playing the violin with one string. His criminal career as a professional burglar began later. He first killed in 1872. Apparently, he eluded capture in a wonderful manner, assuming many disguises and still committing burglaries. He moved to London and lived under the alias of John Ward. He shot a policeman and attempted suicide. He was betrayed in London by a married woman. He confessed to yet another murder before being executed in Manchester in 1876.

I knew none of this as I sat imprisoned by my assailant. In fact, I laughed when he used the name Peace. I thought it ironic that such a violent man should choose to call himself by the name Peace:

'How did you get in, anyway?' I asked.

'You left the door open,' he replied and laughed. 'You left the door open.'

The reply disturbed me. I knew without a doubt that I had locked the front door behind me as I came into the flat. It doesn't shut properly otherwise. It was as though he was referring to some other door, as though I had unwittingly nudged open an invisible door to some infernal region, enabling him to slip through. It occurred to me that I would never know how to shut this intangible door or worse, that I would never know how to avoid accidentally opening it again, this incorporeal door to hell.

'You've got a cut on your back,' he said. 'It looks quite deep.'

'I want an ashtray,' I said. He passed me the empty Silk Cut packet to use as an ashtray. We both stubbed out our cigarettes in it. In the dim light, I caught sight of a large black shape by the wall. I tried to puzzle out what it was. I thought he might have brought a black bag with him, but it turned out to be the overturned television set.

'Put your hands behind your back so I can tie them.'

'No.'

'You're a bloody nuisance, you are.' He sounded exasperated.

'You might want to tie me up because you're a . . .' I could not bring myself to say the word.

'A pervert.' He finished the sentence for me.

'Yes,' I said.

'How do you know I'm not a poof?'

'You can be what you like,' I answered with a liberalism born out of wariness. 'I don't mind.'

'Look. I'm going to get really angry in a minute. If you don't do what I want, I'm going to knock you spark out and then I will rape you. Give me your hands so I can tie them up.'

'Why?' I stalled for time.

'Because I don't want you to see me stark bollock naked in the bath,' he hissed furiously.

'Well, look at me,' I said indignantly. 'How do you think I feel? I haven't got anything on. I feel terrible like this. Let me go and get a dressing-gown.'

'Let me tie your hands and then I'll get you a nightgown.'

'That's no good,' I said. 'If my hands are tied up I won't be able to get them through the sleeves, will I?' My logic made him change tack.

'How old are you?' he asked.

'Twenty-eight,' I lied. I lied for a reason. That summer, in London, a strangler was on the loose. He was called 'The Whispering Strangler' in the press and he only murdered elderly people. It had already occurred to me that this might be the same man, so I knocked a chunk off my age.

'Come off it. How old are you?'

'All right, fifty-eight if that suits you better.'

'Tell me how old you are.'

'No. You might tell the police.' He laughed.

'I'm hungry,' he announced.

'Let me get you something to eat.' I sounded like a new bride.

'No you won't. Don't move. How much money have you got in the flat?'

'Fifteen pounds.'

'Oh, bloody hell.'

'Well, I'm skint. I'll go and get my purse if you like. It's in the hall.' So many small attempts at escape.

'Don't move. Don't move. I'm going to tie your arms and legs.'

'No. You might rape me.'

How can I rape you if I've tied your legs up? We seemed equally matched for logic.

Suddenly, his tone changed. He became gentle, almost shy, as if trying to be genuinely helpful:

'Do you want me to fuck you?" he asked.

'No!' I replied. I was exhausted, so much so that I almost yielded. I had sat hugged up in his arms for nearly an hour. My body was telling me what a normal thing it would be to do. But I feared he would kill me afterwards. The first birds of the dawn chorus began to sing. He became fierce:

'Look. It's getting light. It's getting light. I won't have time for a bath.' I could hear the agitation in his voice. There were sound, practical reasons why he should not be abroad in daylight. Someone might see him. He might be recognised. Perhaps there were other reasons too why he had to be gone before the day fully broke.

'Let me tie your hands.'

I was so exhausted that I agreed.

'All right then, you can tie them as long as you tie them up in front of me and you don't tie them too tight.'

'Give me the rope then.' I gave it to him.

'Put your hands over your head.' I put my hands over my head for a minute and then put them down again.

'I don't like doing that. It makes me feel frightened. I'll put them over my shoulder.' I put them over my left shoulder, elbows together, hands opened.

'Put your hands together,' he ordered. I closed my hands and opened my elbows.

'Put your elbows together,' he said. I put my elbows together and my hands flat together and I pulled my wrists as far apart as I could. We used to do this as children, playing games of prisoner and captor, to enable a quick escape. All the frightening games of childhood are a preparation for this sort of experience: skirmishes, hunting, tracking games, tying up to a tree games. It's a shame we stop playing them. We get out of practice. He tied my wrists, knotting the rope carefully between them. From the way I had held my wrists, I knew immediately that there was enough leeway for me to be able to slip the bonds when the opportunity arose. I would wait until it became absolutely necessary.

As soon as my wrists were tied he became more savage. In a sudden outburst of violence, he manhandled me towards the bed. That was to be the pattern. The more concessions I made, the more cruel he became. Any weakness from me generated his power. With hindsight, I understand that it is pointless to co-operate with a demon or appeal to his better nature when he has the upper hand.

'Kneel down by the bed. Are you going to do what I say?' He spoke with the same, growling, whispered intensity.

'Yes, sir. No, sir,' I replied, with the cunning obsequiousness of the slave. He held me by the neck while he dragged the woven Mexican blanket off my bed. He draped it over my head and helped me gently to my feet. The blanket hung about two feet over my head. If I held it out in front of me I could see the floor.

'All right. Where's your purse?' He asked.

I walked out into the hallway with him close behind me. I fumbled around on the trunk but couldn't find my purse:

'I can't find it. Let me switch the light on a minute.'

'Don't switch the light on.' The words were spat out. Under the piles of papers and letters on the chest I knew that, somewhere, there was an iron tyre lever. I couldn't risk rummaging around for it. He was too near me. The opportunity slid past like a ship in the night that fails to see the life-raft. I found my purse and opened it. He was still behind me. I felt him come closer. His chin must have been near my shoulder because it was then that I felt his stare. It was a stare of such power and evil that I knew, from that moment, that I must never attempt to look at his face. That was partly prudence. If he knew that I could identify him he would have greater reason to kill. But there was something else. I thought that if I turned, I would see a visage so appalling, so fearful that I would be paralysed with terror. I looked in my purse:

'I'm sorry. There's only ten pounds here.' I handed him the note. I fiddled around in the purse again and found two one pound coins and a fifty pence piece. A stubborn meanness came over me that made me want to keep it:

'You don't want all this small change, do you?' I said confidently, as if that was the end of the matter.

'No,' he acquiesced. I seized the advantage.

'You know when your mouth goes all dry because you're frightened,' I said. 'Well, that's how my mouth's gone. I want a glass of water.' Tentatively, I began to call the shots. We walked back along the hall and into the kitchen. The blanket was still over my head. He stayed close behind me. With tied hands I reached for a glass from the shelf over the sink and poured myself a glass of water:

'Do you want some?' I asked.

'No.' I felt him jerk back like a man with hydrophobia. On the draining-board, next to the sink, lay a large Sabatier kitchen knife. My thoughts ran here and there like a rat in a cul-de-sac. I could make a grab for the knife but he might overpower me and use it against me. He was being cooperative at this moment, perhaps it would be better not to antagonise him. But finally, it was the desire to kill that was lacking in me. I let it be, hoping that he had not seen the knife.

Of course, he had seen it.

'What food have you got?' he enquired.

'There's some bread.' I opened the big cupboard and took out a green plastic carrier-bag. Into it I put the remains of a loaf from the bread-bin. On the fridge were three nectarines.

'Why don't you have some of those, they're nice,' I said, sounding like a shop assistant at a greengrocer's.

'What are they? Plums?'

'No. They're nectarines.' I hoped that didn't sound too fancy.

'I'll leave you one for your breakfast,' he said.

'Thanks.' I opened the fridge door, crouched on the floor, the blanket covering my head. The fridge was nearly empty.

'Blimey, there's not much here. There's only a bit of cucumber. Do you want it?'

'No.'

He began to push me towards the bathroom. He picked up a chair from the kitchen:

'I'll take this chair so you've got something to sit on.'

'It's all right. There's one in there,' I said.

In the bathroom he told me to keep the blanket over my head and stand still. He switched on the light. Then he took some books and papers off the chair so that I would be more comfortable. The chair was beside the wash-basin, facing the toilet. I sat down. For the first time, I began to feel sick. Bathrooms are dangerous places to fight in. There are too many hard edges. I thought he was going to run the water in the bath and drown me, or push my head down the toilet bowl and murder me that way. I leaned forward and put the toilet lid down. That would delay him another second or two:

'I'll sit on the toilet seat,' I said.

'No you won't. Don't move.' He didn't want me seated behind him while he was facing the sink in case I saw him in the mirror of the cabinet. I could not see what he was doing. I just heard sounds. I heard the water running in the basin. He seemed to be doing something with his gloves. He asked for soap. I told him where it was. Whatever he was doing, he was doing it carefully and methodically. He asked for a comb. I heard him combing his hair for a long time, slowly, ritualistically. It was then I knew for certain he was no ordinary burglar. I think he used one of my towels. Then he took a damp cloth, lifted the blanket from behind and washed the wound on my back. When he had finished in the bathroom, he announced that we would go and get my dressing-gown. We walked down the hall and into the big bedroom. I was relieved to be out of the bathroom.

'Where is it?' he asked.

'Do you see that wardrobe?' From under the blanket I managed to indicate the walk-in wardrobe. 'Well, it's hanging on the inside of the door.' He walked round the bed towards the wardrobe.

'Has it got flowers on it?' he asked, sounding innocent.

'Yes.'

He stood behind me and lifted the blanket from my head. Tenderly, he placed the dressing-gown round my shoulders. I felt the roughness of his gloves. He draped the blanket back over my head.

'Do you want me to button up the front for you?' he asked.

'No.'

'Now I am going to tie your feet up. Do you want to lie on the bed or do you want to lie on the floor?'

'I don't want you to tie my feet up. I don't like having my feet tied. It's horrible.' I shifted the blanket a little.

'Don't move that blanket about.'

'I can't help it. It's hot under here. I can't breathe.'

'They all say that,' he replied, coldly.

We argued for a while. He told me to sit down on the bed. The bed is just a base with a mattress on it, covered by a red woollen blanket. It is low on the ground. He told me not to move and he left the room. The full-length curtains were drawn. There was not much light. He returned almost immediately and offered me another of my cigarettes. I held the blanket away from me and he reached down and lit it for me. I could see the silver-coloured metal lighter. It was the old-fashioned sort with a flip-top, hinged on the short side. This time he did not smoke. He knew how to wait.

'I need another ashtray,' I said. He accompanied me back into the kitchen. I couldn't see an ashtray. I took a small plate and we returned to the bedroom where I finished my cigarette.

'I'm going to tie your feet.' He became aggressive. I grumbled but exhaustion had weakened my will. I sat on the end of the bed and he tied up my feet. He tied them skilfully, kneeling on the floor a little to my left. He tied both feet at the ankles, and knotted the rope in between. I felt miserably powerless. Although I knew I could free my hands when necessary, my feet had been bound too fast for me to loosen the ties.

'You've got hairy legs,' he sneered.

'That's no way to speak to a friend,' I retorted. I used the word 'friend' deliberately, so that he might find it more difficult to kill me. Suddenly, I had a vision of my blood-stained body, lying undiscovered for days. He gave his chuckling grunt:

'Your feet are tiny,' he said, as if to apologise.

He left the room and I heard him go into the kitchen. Moments later, he returned. He stood directly in front of me and thrust a big knife under the blanket. It was the Sabatier kitchen knife. He had taken off his gloves.

'I've got a big knife here. Can you see it? Can you see it?' The voice was fierce and powerful.

'Yes.' His trousers were lowered to just below the top of his thighs. He had an erection.

'You said you wouldn't do this,' I said, sulkily.

'Well, I am,' he replied, spitefully. 'Are you going to do what I say? Yes or no? YES OR NO?'

'I suppose so,' I grumbled.

'Now then, I want you to suck me off.' The blade of the knife was a dull grey under the blanket. A perverse feeling of obstinacy came over me.

'Well, I don't know how to do that,' I said. He seemed bewildered by the reply.

'You just put it in your mouth and suck,' he explained.

'Well, I can't. I don't know how to.' I was careful not to insult him sexually.

'Kneel down by the side of the bed,' he said in a harsh growl. I knelt down facing the bed. 'Lie on your stomach on the bed.' I didn't move. He began to pull at my legs. I was feeling annoyed. I did not cooperate. Eventually he pulled me on to the bed.

'Lie flat and put your arms above your head.'

All my instincts told me not to lie prone. I raised myself on my elbows. If he used the knife I had to be ready.

'Lie flat.'

'No. I'm all right like this.' He was kneeling behind me.

'I'm going to feel you,' he said. He began to fondle my breasts gently and firmly. It was almost pleasurable – if death had not been on my mind. Murder.

'Now I'm going to rub myself against you.' He pushed the blanket and dressing-gown up my back and put his arms underneath my arms. His hands were flat on the bed. For the first time, I was able to see his hands. They were neat, well-proportioned, unremarkable hands, clean with a fine covering of fairish hair. He began to rub his erect penis between the cheeks of my behind. I peeked out from under the blanket to see if I could locate the knife. No sign of it. But I knew that as long as I could see his hands he couldn't use the weapon.

'Sit back on the bed.' I did what he said.

'Right. Now suck me off.'

Thrust under the blanket, his erect penis floated in the air, flanked by two smooth, round balls. I wondered if they were swollen from when I had grabbed them earlier in the fight. I considered biting the penis or freeing my hands and tearing at the genitals, but I did not know where he had put the knife. One thing I did know. I was not going to suck him off.

'I can't. I don't know how to,' I repeated.

'Why won't you suck me off?' he asked, plaintively, a little hurt. I got stubborn. The dynamics of childishness entered into the situation. Cussedness took hold of me.

'Don't want to,' I said.

'Why not?' he complained.

Here was a dilemma. I couldn't say 'Because you're a fucking maniac,' so I bargained.

'I might toss you off,' I said.

'Go on then.'

I rubbed my hands up and down his penis and touched his balls. Then, as women often do, I got bored and stopped.

'I can't do this. It's too difficult with my hands tied.'

'Well squeeze it then.'

I squeezed it unenthusiastically for a second or two and stopped. There was a pause.

'Lie back on the bed. Keep the blanket over your face. I'm going to come over your tits.'

He was forced to do it himself. I lay back and after a while he ejaculated over and between my breasts. It felt warm. He took a cloth which he must have brought with him and wiped me thoroughly. I glimpsed the sleeve of a leather jacket and the slightly worn cuff of a dark nylon sweater. Then he said, quietly:

'It's all over.'

What did he mean? Life?

He left the bedroom and returned quickly. I had sat up on the edge of the bed, the blanket still over my head. He knelt down and cut the rope between my ankles. As he did so, he nicked me with the knife.

'Ouch,' I said.

'Sorry,' he said.

'Thanks,' I said.

'Where's your telephone? Where's your telephone?' He sounded panicky.

'It's in the front room.'

'Where is it exactly?'

'If you go into the front room, it's on the floor over to the left.'

'I'm going to cut the wires.' Suddenly, he began to rummage around among some packages that had been left on the bed from the night before.

'Where's me food bag? Where's me food bag? What's in these bags?' he asked.

'Soap and stuff that someone's taking to my family abroad for me.'

He left the room and I heard his footsteps retreating down the hall. For two seconds I hesitated. Then I quickly freed my hands, keeping them hidden under the blanket lest he returned. I waited for one more second and threw the blanket from my head. I ran across the room to the back window, pushed back the curtain and with one manoeuvre, opened the window. I leapt out into the back garden. The air was chill. I jumped up the four stone steps onto the wet grass. I was exhilarated. Yelling for the people upstairs, I raced across the grass to the fence, scratching myself on the rose bushes. I tried to climb onto the fence but fell back. Then, with one enormous effort, I was on top of the fence with its three foot-high trellis. I was still naked. Naked and free. It was early dawn. Everywhere was quiet and still. I glanced back at the window to see if a figure was climbing out in pursuit of me and I yelled with the power of an opera singer. I was half-caught in the branches of a pear tree, an early morning goddess, calling and hollering. Slowly, neighbours came to various windows:

'Quick! Get the police.' My voice was huge and clear. Soon the police arrived. There was no sign of the man.

For the first two days afterwards, the police were consideration itself. A plump, brown-haired policewoman was assigned to my case and spent most of the first day taking down my statement. Then she drove me to a friend's house where I was to stay the night while my flat was sealed off for forensic examination. I was, naturally, exhausted. Before I fell asleep, words from the twenty-third psalm floated into my head. I remembered something about lying down in green pastures and walking beside still waters. Suddenly, I experienced the sensation of walking through delightful pastures of long green grass dotted with yellow wild flowers until I came and stood by the stillest of waters. At the same time, my own physical boundaries dissolved and I recognised that those green meadows and rivers were inside me. The experience was so full of wonder that I tried to delay going to sleep in order to prolong it, but soon I fell into the most profound and peaceful of slumbers. I dreamed. I dreamed the dream of the leopard. The leopard was sitting at one end of my hallway. He was half-painting and half-real. At the other end of the passage was a mirror. The leopard was out of alignment with the mirror. He had to be moved so that he could see in the mirror. But I knew that when he was face to face with the mirror, something terrible would happen. Then I woke up.

On the third day the police turned nasty.

'Mrs Atkins, are you sure you didn't know this intruder? We cannot find a point of entry. Are you sure you didn't let him in?'

'I think he must have got in through the front window. I usually keep it locked but I had a friend staying. She might have opened it.'

'And our forensic people have not been able to find a trace of him. There are no fingerprints and we can't even pick up a footprint. Where is the knife he used?'

'He must have taken it with him.'

'And the cloth he used to wipe you down?'

'He must have taken that too.'

'What about the rope he tied you with?'

'It doesn't seem to be here.' (Later, fortunately, I found the rope that had tied my hands, in the garden.)

'Look. We can see that something happened here. We can see there's been a fight of some sort, but it's very unusual for someone to stay this long in a flat and to have been in the bathroom, the kitchen, the hall, both bedrooms and not leave a trace or a clue behind. Where's the comb he used? We might be able to get one of his hairs from that.'

'It's gone.'

'Did he eat anything?' Use any cutlery? We might be able to get a saliva trace.'

'What about the cigarette stubs?' I suggested. 'We both smoked a cigarette and stubbed them out in an empty packet. There should be a saliva trace on there.'

'That's already been checked. There was only one stub in the packet and that has your saliva on it.'

'He must be very clever,' I said. 'He's taken all the evidence with him.'

Over the next few days my imagination ran wild over the grid of facts, along the boundaries of reason and unreason that are stalked by the ancient figure of fear. Could it have been part of myself that escaped and attacked me? Had the spirit of a nineteenth-century murderer and cabaret artist entered a contemporary small-time burglar? Did we all overlap? Some months later a young plain-clothes detective appeared at the front door:

'Can I come in?' he said. 'I think we've found your man. Would you mind if I brought a police photographer in with me to take some pictures of the flat?'

He leaned nonchalantly against the kitchen door, drinking a coffee while his colleague took photographs of the other rooms:

'You're a performer, I hear. I used to be an actor myself. I was at Hornchurch Repertory Company for nearly a year. Then I gave it up for this.' His collar-length hair still looked actorish. He continued 'Anyway, we're pretty certain it's him, although it's going to be difficult to prove in court with so little evidence. He may well get off. We think it's him that raped another woman near here. We haven't got a scrap of evidence on that either. He's cunning. Spent two nights at her house with putty softener, then removed a whole pane of glass. He's got a history of this sort of thing. Often attacks on Christmas Day. Clever, you see. He's denying it, mind you. Denying everything. I almost felt sorry for him when I was talking to him. He's in a horrendous mental state. Says someone is trying to get into him and tell him what to do. Someone called John, he says. Maybe, it's this John we should be going after. Don't know him do you?' he asked, jokingly.

Charlie Peace, I thought. Alias John Ward. Betrayed by a married woman in London.

'Don't forget you've got the piece of rope I found in the garden,' I said.

'We're not likely to forget that,' he said. 'It's all we have got.'

In court, the man was not in my direct line of vision and he remained turned slightly away from me. Only once did he look at me, as I was demonstrating to the jury how I had held my wrists apart as he tied them. His head swivelled slowly through an angle of one hundred and eighty degrees like an owl, and he stared with great, blank eyes. It was then that I noticed his camel-hair coat and cheap jewellery and a black nylon roll-neck sweater of the type worn by spivs.

THE GIRL WITH THE CELESTIAL LIMB

It is a fact of life that what you run from fastest is what you are most likely to encounter or, to put it another way, what you fear most is what you unknowingly rush headlong to meet. The bizarre story of Jane Cole is an illustration of this. To understand it you must first know a little about her background.

Jane Cole lived with her parents and younger brother in the outer suburbs of London between Mottingham and New Eltham. She was a blonde, square-faced child, unexceptional in every way except for the precocious talent in mathematics which ensured her a place at Eltham Hill Grammar School. There she did well until three days after her fourteenth birthday when she developed a terror of infinity. Quite simply, her mother had asked her to post a letter. The winter evening was clear and cold and she ran up the hill, hair flying, running for no other reason than the excess of energy common in fourteen year olds. She shoved the letter in the slot, flicked back her hair and turned to walk back down the hill. Breathless from running and suffering a slight stitch in her side, she halted and looked up at the sky. There was no time to protect herself from the infinite blackness and the appalling, unintelligible hieroglyphics formed by the stars. Her heart pounded at the awful vastness, the unending, pathless horror of it. She calculated that what she saw stretched without measure and that in relation to it she was the merest speck or atom, destined to be swallowed in this limitless void. Her mouth went dry. Her limbs refused to move and she was rooted to the pavement. Taken unawares, she had caught a glimpse of the meaning of infinity. For a full minute she remained paralysed. Then she lowered her eyes to the pavement and walked back home into the safe, orange cube of light which was the kitchen where her mother was handing out plates of tomatoes on toast. She told no one what had happened.

From then on, Jane Cole took a conscious decision to pursue dullness and mediocrity in all things. The academic spinsters who sat over coffee, discussing their pupils in the staff-room, noted the falling-off in Jane Cole's performance. The English teacher remarked that her vocabulary was shrinking rather than expanding and cruelly nicknamed her after her favourite phrase – 'Dunno really'. The maths teacher, disappointed in her prodigy, recalled one violent row in the classroom over whether or not parallel lines met at infinity, in which her star pupil's former abilities reappeared briefly before she ran out of the class and sat sulking in the cloakroom. The staff had noticed often how girls from the poorer backgrounds arrived at school aged eleven, full of promise, and come puberty lost their intellectual drive, began to hitch up their skirts, open the top button of their blouses and loll around the bus-stop waiting for the boys to come out. Generally, it was assumed she had just burnt herself out.

At the first possible opportunity Jane left school and found herself work in a drab little hairdressing salon in north London. The sign outside read 'SHAPES IN HAI', the R having fallen off some years previously. The clientele was elderly. The proprietor, sixty-year-old Mr Denby, wore comforting beige cardigans with brown wooden buttons and crouched at his desk in the window all day doing crosswords or watching the portable television set at his side.

Jane, her own hair pinned back at the nape, learned to trim, rinse, blow-dry, fix permanent waves, flick the blue nylon capes over the clients – not that there were many – and dodge the sharp tang of the aerosol sprays. She enjoyed the cloyingly sweet smells of the shampoos and the styling mousse. But what she liked best was the banality of the conversations: illnesses, pets, knitting patterns, the occasional article in one of the dog-eared magazines kept for customers, the price of bus fares.

Summer came and with the warmer weather the door of the salon remained open so that passers-by caught whiffs of the odours of hair-setting lotions and glanced in at the rows of driers and the uneventful interior of the parlour where time passed more slowly than on the street. Mr Denby offered her the flat over the shop if she would open up the salon for him three days a week. She accepted and moved in.

One hazy day in August, Jane Cole took her sandwiches and went to sit on the grass of a nearby park during her lunch-break. The park was nearly empty. On a day like this when the sky was glazed, Jane could allow herself to look up. Overhead an aeroplane flew low, making the sound of cloth ripping slowly and unevenly. Another, more distant and at right angles to it, flew in a higher plane, two grey sharks lazing in a muggy sky. Idly, Jane began to work out their relative speeds. Then she turned and noticed a man looking at her from about twenty feet away. There was something odd about his position. With his left hand he held onto the slender trunk of a sapling recently planted by the council, his feet tucked into the base so that he leaned out at an angle. Suddenly he let himself swing gracefully round, anti-clockwise, swapping hands mid-swing so that he grasped the tree with his right hand, ending up at the same angle on the other side. He raised his hat to her.

Immediately, Jane gathered her things and set off to walk back to the salon. As she passed the man she saw that he had a pale and beautifully symmetrical face, the face of an aesthete with a long aquiline nose and eyes set slightly too close together. An elegant gaberdine raincoat hung on a slender body. His gaze was mocking and inquisitive. He smiled as she went by. Three riffs of a Miles Davis number she had heard once on the radio and tried to put out of her head, started up again in her brain.

That afternoon, to her great satisfaction, Jane Cole got by on the following phrases:

'Oh what a shame.'

'The same rinse as last time.'

'Good afternoon.'

'Is that drier too hot for you?'

'I know. I know.'

'That's all right.'

'Fancy.'

The same evening, a huge red sun sank behind the outline of the rooftops opposite leaving a pinky-grey dusk. Jane looked from her window to see if the chip shop on the corner was still open.

There he was again.

This time he executed the same peculiar swing round the lamp-post on the other side of the street but did not seem to be looking in her direction. Jane frowned. Behind the greasy rectangle of light that was the chip shop window she could see the misty figures beginning to pack up for the night. Either she went now or she missed her supper. She ran down the lino-covered stairs. As she stepped into the street, the man twirled and waved his hat. At that moment she felt a pricking in the toe of her right foot as if she had a stone in her shoe. She hobbled to the shop and bought her cod and chips. By the time she left, the whole of her right foot was pricking painfully as if the shoe was filled with thistles. She came to a halt. In the light of the street-lamp she could see the concern in his eyes:

'May I be of assistance?'

The man appeared so genuinely concerned, so anxious to help, that she let him take her arm along the street. Now she could not even put the foot on the ground for the sharp jabbing pains. She leaned on him as they climbed the stairs. At the front door of her flat she hesitated. The man whipped out a card from his pocket:

'Let me present myself,' he said. The card read:

J.F. WIDDERSHINS
GEOMETER
AND
MAKER OF DIVIDERS
AND POLYHEDRAL SUNDIALS

The pain was now so acute that she was powerless to do anything but turn the key in the lock and let them in. He took her weight and helped her over to the divan bed by the window. Jane had done nothing since she moved in to make the flat more homely. The bed sagged under a coverlet whose pattern had wilted and faded. There was a tiny Belling stove in the corner next to the sink, two ugly wooden armchairs and a table with a blue and white chequered formica top. He fetched the stool for her leg.

'I think we'd better take a look at that leg,' he said. He bent over, his shiny chestnut hair glinting in the fading light. Jane felt safe with him, grateful for his presence. With long, tapering fingers he deftly undid the laces of her ankle-boot and gently removed it. Then, with the utmost delicacy, he began to roll down the white knee sock:

'Ah!' he said as he did so. 'A classically beautiful leg if I may say so.'

Jane stared at her leg. From just below the indentation left by the elasticated top of the sock, her leg no longer consisted of flesh and blood. Instead, she found herself looking at the most dazzlingly intricate, three-dimensional network of geometrical shapes. The leg was transparent. Beneath it she could see the yellow plastic seat of the stool. It seemed to have been drawn in mid-air with the finest of pencils. The diagrammatic leg retained the same outline as before and she could distinguish the toe-nails now transformed into a complex of polygons. The main parts of the foot and leg, however, were made up of a web of delicately interconnecting geometric forms, tessellations, cub-octahedrons, star-pentagons, rhombic faces (which revolved), cones, triangles and the cubic lattices of crystallography. Shocked and fascinated, Jane stayed dumb.

'Well, well,' said Widdershins, kneeling to inspect the mathematical limb more closely. 'No wonder the shoe and sock were painful – all those acute angles. Has the pain abated somewhat?'

Jane nodded. Widdershins regarded her quizzically:

'You seem surprised. Why is that?' he asked.

Jane searched for the vocabulary she had jettisoned. It failed to arrive:

'Dunno really,' she said.

'Come, come.' His tone was mildly reproving. 'You are one of us. I think you have always known that there is nothing real except mathematics. May I help myself to one of your chips?'

Jane still held the warm, greasy packet of fish and chips to her chest. She opened it and he took one, pulling up one of the armchairs to sit beside her in the evening light:

'I am a pure mathematician. A classicist. The pure mathematician is the only one in direct contact with reality. The reality of pure mathematics lies outside us. The area of a circle is πr^2 not because our minds are shaped one way or another but because it is so, because mathematical reality is built that way. A man who could give a convincing account of mathematical reality would solve the most difficult problems of metaphysics. If he included physical reality in his account, he would have solved them all.'

Widdershins fell into a deep musing, the soggy chip dangling from between his fingers. Jane Cole looked out of the window to check that the street was still there. Nothing had changed. A fat dog waddled by. Widdershin's presence unexpectedly soothed her, his manner was calming and the sight of her leg, far from disturbing her, only seemed to re-affirm something she had known, albeit hazily, since she was a young child. Besides, the leg was astoundingly beautiful. She altered the position of her foot. Immediately, the complex pattern of forms shifted in the manner of a kaleidoscope.

'Ahhhhhh,' said Widdershins, opening his eyes and observing the leg once more. 'The exquisite double helix. And look! Kepler's stella octangula.'

He pulled out a handkerchief and wiped his hands fastidiously with it: 'I wonder if I might ask a favour of you. Do you think I might call on another acquaintance of mine to come and have a look at this?'

'Certainly,' said Jane, beginning to enjoy the attention.

Widdershins moved swiftly to lift up the wonky sash window. He leaned out and gave a melodious whistle. Straightaway, a figure detached itself from the shadows of the building opposite and came leaping across the road. Jane heard footsteps bounding up the stairs two at a time. Into the room burst a tall, gangly young man with a shock of yellow hair. He wore a black and red check lumberjacket shirt of brushed cotton and black jeans. Holding up his arms like a singer acknowledging cheers he gave an extravagant off-centre bow and announced himself:

'Hoodlum. Rock and roller. Anarcho-syndicalist and collector of irrational numbers, OK? What's going on then? Do I smell chips or do I not smell chips?'

He came over to grab some chips from the packet proffered by Jane. She smelt the sweat as he reached out his arm.

'Whoop de doop doop doop! What have we here?' he crowed as he spotted the leg.'

'I thought you might be interested,' said Widdershins modestly.

Jane fixed her hair back from her eyes. Events this far beyond her control allowed her a delicious irresponsibility. She waggled her toes and watched the ensuing transformation of the geometrical pattern. Hoodlum goggled at the permutating shank. It was getting dark. He walked round the leg to view it from another angle.

'I can fuck that leg up,' said Hoodlum suddenly.

'I think not,' said Widdershins, on the defensive.

'I can fuck it up numerically.'

Widdershins frowned. 'How?'

'See that little square.' He pointed to a tiny perfect square just below the little toe. 'Measure it,' he challenged Widdershins. Widdershins took out a pair of dividers and a tape from his pocket.

'One centimetre each side,' he said.

'Gotcha!' yelled Hoodlum. 'Look at the leg numerically for a minute.'

Jane regarded Hoodlum with amazement. The whites of his eyes, white as school milk, bulged and the dark centres were spinning. Immediately, she experienced a tingling in her leg. She looked down and flinched. The leg appeared to be swarming with ants. On closer inspection she saw that it was a seething mass of miniature numerals and tiny black multiplication, addition and minus signs all marching in file through the density of her leg and turning over with incredible rapidity.

'The exact numerical representation of your geometry,' said Hoodlum triumphantly to Widdershins. 'Which means that the diagonal of your one centimetre-sided square is the square root of two. An irrational number. It don't exist,' hooted Hoodlum.

Even in the dim light, Jane could see that Widdershins had gone pale.

'You've made a hole in her leg,' he said in alarm.

Jane began to feel faint. Where the square had been, just below her little toe, the numbers were falling off into nowhere. Widdershins hurried to the door:

'I'll have to get Afreet.' He vanished down the stairs.

'Who's Afreet?' she asked.

'A mechanic,' said Hoodlum. 'Can I have this fish?'

He gobbled down the fish before she could reply. Then he leapt into the middle of the room, miming playing the guitar, and sang raucously:

'Goodbyeeee Google-eyeeee.'

Jane thought he was good-looking. She tried to look vulnerable:

'Do you think I'll die?' she asked.

'Fuck knows,' said Hoodlum.

Jane chanced another squint at her leg. The numbers were not falling off into nowhere. They were falling onto the floor in a little heap like iron filings.

'I'd like my leg back to normal. I have to stand up all day.'

'All day and all of the night,' sang Hoodlum.

Suddenly, Hoodlum was all over her, plastering her face and neck with ecstatic wet kisses.

'Mind my leg,' she said, enjoying the roughness of his shirt rubbing up against her.

'I can fuck you without touching that leg,' boasted Hoodlum, which was exactly what he was doing, while she kept an eye on the mounting pile of numbers on the floor next to the stool.

Two voices could be heard coming up the stairs. Hoodlum got up and did up his jeans:

Widdershins opened the door, switched on the light and ushered in a short man, not more than three feet high with an enormous head covered in frizzy, electric hair. He carried a tool-bag:

'Right, now.' His manner was slow and practical. 'I'm the quantum mechanic. Where's the trouble?'

'Over here.' Widdershins gestured elegantly in the direction of Jane. 'This young lady has developed a hole which is, I'm afraid, beyond repair by classical means.'

Hoodlum blushed and began to whistle. Afreet went over to the wash-basin and stood on tiptoe to wash his hands. Then he came over to the bed:

'Let's have a look. No need to get upset, miss,' he said at the sight of Jane, who was looking a bit rumpled.

His broad forehead wrinkled as he studied the leg:

'I see what you mean. Well, you've been looking at it the wrong way. It's always the same with you pure mathematicians, if you don't mind my saying so. Airy-fairy idealists. I'm a nuts and bolts man myself.'

A pained expression passed over Widdershin's refined face. Hoodlum scuffed his feet.

'Well, you'll have to look at it my way. I know you don't like it, Mr Widdershins, but that's all there is to it.'

'Hurry up, please,' said Jane.

'Now I'm not one to be hurried, miss. In fact, I like to take my time and explain things as I go along so everyone's in the picture.' As he spoke, Afreet rummaged in his tool-bag. He took out a geiger-counter, a tin box with the word 'photons' written on it in felt-tip pen and the parts of what looked like a telescope, which he proceeded to assemble. When he had done this he sat down in the chair next to Jane.

'Now miss, you know that you are nothing but a mass of jigging electrons and sub-atomic particles, don't you?' he said, patting her kindly on the hand. Jane nodded doubtfully. Her leg was itching. Afreet continued:

'It's an ancient idea. Democritus had it in 420 BC. He decided that when you cut an apple, the knife finds out the spaces between the atoms. Not far wrong. Leibnitz was another one. An atomist.' Hoodlum gave a loud yawn which Afreet disregarded. 'Leibnitz would have thought of that table over there as a colony of souls. Sometimes, when I'm feeling a bit romantic, I think of myself as a soul-tailor,' he added sheepishly.

Hoodlum, showing major signs of jealousy, let out a loud guffaw. Widdershins shut him up with a glance.

'As I was saying, matter is just a handy way of collecting atomic and sub-atomic events into packages. And now we're going to examine your leg in that light.'

'Couldn't you put me to sleep with an anaesthetic?' asked Jane, quailing at the thought.

' 'Fraid not, miss. Consciousness is crucial in quantum mechanics. You'll have to observe your leg. Unless you see it, it won't be there, so to speak. Even the tiniest electron can't really be said to exist until there's an observer, let alone a whopping great leg.'

Widdershins could no longer contain himself: 'But surely, at some level quantum physics turns into classical physics?'

'Who said?' snapped Afreet.

'Surely the world enjoys an independent existence, an objective reality in accordance with certain classical laws which it obeys whether there is anyone to observe them or not?' said Widdershins.

'It did, Mr Widdershins, until quantum mechanics came along. Now everything's atoms. Reality is a fuzzy business, Mr Widdershins. I see with my eyes, which are a collection of whirling atoms, through the light, which is a collection of whirling atoms. What do I see? I see you, Mr Widdershins, who are also a collection of whirling atoms. And in all this intermingling of atoms who is to know where anything starts and anything stops. It's an atomic soup we're in, Mr Widdershins. And all these quantum limbo states only collapse into one concrete reality when there is a human observer. Like the young lady here. Now then. We have a leg here that is dripping numbers. Do you want me to try and deal with it or not?'

Jane held her hands over her eyes. Widdershins was unable to leave well alone: 'Einstein,' he said loftily, 'believed that there is a reality which we uncover by our observations. He believed in a substratum of deterministic forces that drive the unpredictable hi-jinks of your electrons. He just happened to die before they were discovered.'

The mention of the name Einstein seemed to throw Afreet into a frenzy. He stood up and banged his tool-bag on the ground. Hoodlum backed off into a corner.

'Einstein,' he growled. 'It was his bloody theory that stopped us finding out about faster-than-light signalling. He didn't know about the conspiracy of particles – what he called "spooky action at a distance". He didn't know about enfolded order – space folding and unfolding. He didn't consider the possibility of multiple universes.' Afreet began to hop up and down:

'LOOK AT THE LEG,' he roared. 'LOOK AT THE LEG.'

Just then, Jane felt the tingling in her leg stop, to be replaced by a sensation of unbearable lightness. She took her hands away from her eyes. Below the knee, her leg had no beginning and no end. She saw clearly the same infinite space, the same dizzying void that she had seen once before on a clear winter's night, the same spiralling galaxies and pendant heavenly bodies that could be either stars or electrons.

Afreet appeared to have recovered his equanimity and was fiddling about with the telescope:

'I think I've got it. I can see the problem way down one end. It's a black hole.' He packed up his telescope. Jane kept her eyes averted from the celestial limb.

'Can you fix it?' enquired Widdershins, anxiously. 'Surely you can. After all, as Einst . . .' He corrected himself. 'As somebody said, ''God may be subtle, but he's not malicious''.' He laughed, nervously.

'That's not my experience, Mr Widdershins. In my experience God is extremely malicious. And the answer is ''No''. I can't fix it. As you well know, it is the point where all laws cease.'

Hoodlum let out a whistle, secretly proud of himself for having fucked a woman who contained such lawlessness.

'The best I can do,' said Afreet, wiping his forehead with a handkerchief, 'is a Schrodinger's cat job. And that only has a fifty-fifty chance of success.'

Widdershins swivelled slowly round on his heels from left to right: 'It's not very satisfactory,' he said.

'It's the best I can do. She'll have a fifty per cent chance of living.'

Turning her head to avoid seeing the vertiginous depth that was her leg, Jane determined to exert some control:

'If I've got to take a risk, I want to know the facts,' she demanded. Patiently, Afreet explained:

'If I don't do something, in twelve hours' time all the atoms of which you are comprised will collapse into that black hole. I can set up a condition whereby either that will happen or you will revert to your former self with your former leg. It's a quantum superposition of two states – alive and dead. You will be both alive and dead at the same time. Only when a human observer comes and looks in the room will you flip definitively into one of the two states. Hopefully, in your case it will be life. Schrodinger designed the experiment for a cat, originally.'

'I don't understand why there needs to be an observer,' said Jane, angrily. Afreet sighed and scratched his bushy head:

'Oh dear, I thought you'd understood. Think of tomorrow's crossword puzzle. The answers to it are already in your head.

But the answers make no sense now, not until the questions are posed. The puzzle brings out one correct answer from the soup of answers in your head. Just the same as the human observer brings out one version of reality.'

'Why can't one of you stay and observe me?'

Widdershins intervened delicately:

'I think that is a question better left aside for the moment.'

'Well what will it be like to be both alive and dead at the same time?'

'Horrible,' said Hoodlum. Widdershins stepped quickly forward nearly tripping over Afreet who was searching for his box of photons.

'I think, my dear, that it would be rather like a dream. You frequently find such duality in dreams and it is not at all unpleasant. You know that someone is both your father and the newsagent simultaneously. In a dream it would feel quite acceptable to be dead and to be weeding the garden at one and the same time. We can leave a note for your boss asking him to come and wake you. I'm afraid that Hoodlum, Afreet and myself are inveterate gamblers. I hope you will not disappoint us by refusing this option.'

'I've got no choice,' said Jane and then added, bitterly: 'I knew mathematics would bring me to this.'

Hoodlum, Widdershins and Afreet looked somewhat abashed. Jane shut her eyes. She heard Afreet whispering something and shutting the tin box. Then the three of them tiptoed out of the room closing the door softly behind them. They left a polite note for Mr Denby explaining that Jane's alarm clock was not working and would he go up and wake her if she was late for her nine o'clock appointment.

At break of day, three figures could be seen walking through the park, one of medium height, one tall and waving his arms about and the other extremely short. They crossed the grass and disappeared into the dawn mist.

Next morning, Mr Denby arrived to find the salon unopened and Mrs Reynolds waiting outside. After reading the note, he climbed up the stairs and knocked at the door of the flat. There was no reply. He let himself in with the master key. There was no sign of Jane Cole. The divan bed had not been slept in. The remains of a fish supper lay on the table. He noticed a white sock

and shoe on the floor next to what looked like a little pile of soot.
Then he went back downstairs.

All morning, in the salon, the talk was about the reliability and
unreliability of young girls.

EAT LABBA AND
DRINK CREEK WATER

Lorna fled from Jamaica and came to lie in my London flat for a year recovering from Philip who had gone back to his wife. She arrived with two bulging suitcases and chicken-pox:

'I can't bear to live on the island while he's there with her.' The tears were extraordinary. They spouted from the outermost corners of her eyes. When she blinked they squirted out. She consumed quantities of Frascati wine and swallowed all the pills my doctor could provide. Sometimes I heard her shouting in her sleep. Every so often she managed to haul herself by train to the provincial university where she was completing a thesis on the sugar riots of the thirties. I imagined her, this white-looking creole girl, jolting along in a British Rail compartment that smelled of stale smoke, weeping and puffing at cigarettes and staring out at the grey English weather which she hated. In the end:

'I'm going back,' she said.

'I'm going back too, to Guyana.'

'Why?'

'I don't know. I want to see my aunts before they die. They're old. And I want to spend some time in Georgetown, in the house with Evelyn and the others. I miss the landscape. Perhaps I'll buy a piece of land there. I don't know why. I just want to go back.'

•   •   •

'Eat labba and drink creek water and you will always return', so the saying goes.

Once I dreamed I returned by walking in the manner of a

high-wire artist, arms outstretched, across a frail spider's thread
suspended sixty feet above the Atlantic attached to Big Ben at
one end and St George's Cathedral, Demerara, at the other. It
took me twenty-two days to do it and during the whole of that
time only the moon shone.

Another time, my dream blew me clean across the ocean like
tumbleweed. That took only three days and the sun and the
moon shone alternately as per usual.

We do return and leave and return again, criss-crossing the
Atlantic, but whichever side of the Atlantic we are on, the
dream is always on the other side.

●   ●   ●

I am splashing in the waters of the lake at Suddie. The waters
are a strange reddish colour, the colour of Pepsi-Cola and
the lake is fenced in with reeds. The sky is a grey-blue lid
with clouds in it – far too big for the lake. Opposite me on
the far side, an Amerindian woman sits motionless in the
back of a canoe wedged in the reeds. She is clutching a
paddle.

They say that the spirit of a pale boy is trapped beneath the
waters of one of the creeks nearby. You can see him looking up
when sunlight penetrates the overhanging branches and green
butterfly leaves, caught between the reflections of tree roots that
stretch like fins from the banks into the water.

●   ●   ●

'So you're going back to the West Indies,' says the man at the
party, in his blue and white striped shirt. 'I was on holiday in
Montego Bay last year. How I envy you. All those white beaches
and palm trees.'

But it's not like that, I think to myself. It's not like that at all. I
think of Jamaica with its harsh sunlight and stony roads.
Everything is more visible there, the gunmen, the politics, the
sturdy, outspoken people. And I think of the Guyanese coast,
with its crab-infested mud-flats and low trees dipping into the
water.

'You've got all that wonderful reggae music too,' the man is saying. But I don't bother to put him right because the buzz of conversation is too loud.

•   •   •

The pale boy's name is Wat. He is standing on the deck of a ship at anchor in the estuary of a great river, screwing up his eyes to scan the coast. The boards of the deck are burning hot underfoot. The sun pulverises his head. His father, leader of the expedition, comes over to him and puts his hand on the boy's shoulder:

'At last we have found entry into the Guianas,' he says.

Wat's heart beats a little faster. This is it. Somewhere in the interior they will find Manoa which the Spaniards call El Dorado. They will outdo the feats of Cortes and Pizarro. They will discover

The mountain of crystal

The empire where there is more abundance of gold than in Peru

The palaces that contain feathered fish, beasts and birds, all fashioned in gold by men with no iron implements

The pleasure gardens with intricate replicas of trees, herbs and flowers, all wrought in silver and gold.

He gazes eagerly ahead. There is mud, green bush, river and more bush stretching as far as the eye can see. And there are no seagulls. Unlike the coast of England where the birds had shrieked them such a noisy farewell, this coast is utterly silent.

•   •   •

The body of an Amerindian is falling through the mists, a brown leaf curling and twisting downwards until it reaches the earth with a thud like fruit.

•   •   •

A low mournful hoot signals the departure of the SS *Essequibo* as it steams out of the Demerara into the Atlantic.

A young man of twenty-one braces himself against the rail taking deep breaths of the future. There is not much of the African left in his appearance, a hint of it perhaps in the tawny colour of a complexion mixed over generations with Scottish, Amerindian and Portuguese. He lets go of the rail and strolls towards the prow of the ship. His eyes never leave the horizon. Not once does he look back as the land recedes away behind him, because

In England there is a library that contains all the books in the world, a cathedral of knowledge the interior of whose dome shimmers gold from the lettering on spines of ancient volumes.

In England there are theatres and concert halls and galleries hung from ceiling to floor with magnificent gold-framed paintings and all of these are peopled by men in black silk opera hats and women with skins like cream of coconut.

In England there are museums which house the giant skeletons of dinosaurs whose breastbones flute into a rib-cage as lofty and vast as the stone ribs inside Westminister Abbey, which he has seen on a postcard.

This is what will happen.

He will disembark in the industrial docks of Liverpool to the delicious shock of seeing, for the first time, white men working with their hands.

For a year he will study law at the Inns of Court in London.

In the Great War of Europe, two of the fingers of his left hand will be torn off by shrapnel. A bluish wound will disfigure the calf of his leg. The thundering of the artillery will render him stone deaf in one ear and after a period of rehabilitation in Shorncliffe, Kent, he will be returned to his native land where his mother, brothers and sisters wait for him on the verandah. He brings with him a letter signed by the King of England which his mother frames and hangs in the living-room. It says:

'A Grateful Mother Country Thanks You For Your Sacrifice.'

•   •   •

They are drenched with spray, Wat, his father and six of the crew, clinging to the rocks at the base of the giant falls of Kaeitur, a waterfall so enormous that it makes the sound of a thousand bells as the column of water falls thousands of feet to the River Potaro below. Each one of them is exhausted, but above all, perplexed. For two weeks they have travelled up river led by an Arawak guide. Before they set off they explained carefully to him through an interpreter that they were seeking the mountain of crystal. And this is where he has brought them.

·   ·   ·

'I'm coming on November the sixth,' I yell down the phone to Evelyn. 'I'll go to see my aunts in New Amsterdam for a couple of days then I'll come and stay with you.'

'That is good.' Evelyn's voice is faint and crackly. 'Bring a Gestetner machine with you. They need one at the party headquarters. Really we need a computer but that costs thousands of dollars. We'll pay you for it when you reach.'

'OK Evelyn. I'll see you in two weeks' time. I can't wait. Bye.'

'Bye. Don' forget ink and paper.'

I lie back on the bed wiggling my toes and thinking of Evelyn. She is a stockily-built black woman of thirty-six, a financial wizard in the pin-ball economy of the country. She will never leave. Her house is set back a little from the road. On every side of its white-painted exterior, tiers of Demerara shutters open, bottom out, stiff sails designed to catch the least breath of wind. I try to imagine whereabouts she is in the house. She has a cordless telephone now so she could be anywhere – in the kitchen perhaps or wandering about upstairs. When the Trade Winds blow the upper floors of the house are full of air encrusted with salt and at night the house creaks like a ship resting at anchor in the city of wooden dreams, a city built on stilts, belonging neither to land nor to sea but to land reclaimed from the sea.

·   ·   ·

Beneath his father's framed certificate from the King of England, a slim youth of nineteen leans his back against the dresser thinking:

'If I don't get out of this colony I shall suffocate.'

A problem has arisen over his leaving. His father and Mr Wilkinson, his employer, are discussing it in the stifling inertia of mid-day. His father is frowning and flexing the stubs of his two fingers, as if they have pins and needles. Mr Wilkinson is one of those gingery, peppery Englishmen whose long stay in the tropics has sucked all the moisture from him, leaving a dry sandy exterior. He too is frowning at the piece of paper in his hand.

'The trouble is with this damn birth certificate. The transfer to London went through all right. The Booker-McConnell people in London agreed to it, then, out of the blue, they ask for his birth certificate. Just a formality I suppose. All the same . . .'

His voice tails off into silence.

On the birth certificate, under the section marked 'Type' are written the words: 'Coloured. Native. Creole.'

The young man's eyes are solemn and watchful as he waits for his elders to find a solution. He has a recurring nightmare which is this: that Crab Island, the chunk of mud and jungle in the estuary of the Berbice River, grows to such enormous proportions that it blocks forever his escape from New Amsterdam; that he is forced to stay in the stultifyingly dull town with its straggly cabbage palms and telegraph poles whose wires carry singing messages from nowhere to nowhere. He awakes from the dream sweating and in a claustrophobic panic.

In London there is jazz and the Café Royal.

In London you can skate across the Thames when it is frozen and there is snow snow snow in a million crystal flakes.

In London there are debonair, sophisticated, cosmopolitan men. It is impossible to *be* a real man until you have been to London.

He watches them sip their rum punches by the window. In the silence, music drifts up from the phonograph playing in the bottom-house:

> The music goes round and round
> Oh oh oh, Oh oh oh
> And it comes out here.

Gazing at the three of them with blank disdainful eyes is the portrait of an Amerindian.

Mr Wilkinson continues, embarrassed:

'Frankly, I don't expect it will make any difference, but I wouldn't like there to be any foul-up at this late stage. I'll tell you what we'll do. Have you got his baptism certificate? They don't put all this rubbish on the baptism certificate. I'll write a letter to London saying the birth certificate was destroyed by a fire in the records office. I'll enclose the baptism certificate instead. That should fix it. They won't bother once he's there.' He takes another swallow of his drink. 'I suppose they have to be careful. It is the City of London after all, where they set the Gold Standard for the world.' He winks.

●　　　　●　　　　●

The great and golden city is to be discovered in the heart of a large, rich and beautiful empire. The city is well proportioned and has many great towers. Throughout, there are laid out goodly gardens and parks, some of them containing ponds of excellent fish. There are, too, many squares where trading is done and markets are held for the buying and selling of all manner of wares: ornaments of gold, silver, lead, brass and copper; game, birds of every species, rabbits, hares and partridges; vegetables, fish and fruit.

In all the districts of this great city are many temples or houses for their idols.

In one part of the city they have built cages to house large numbers of lions, tigers, wolves, foxes and cats of various kinds.

There are yet other large houses where live many men and women with deformities and various maladies. Likewise there are people to look after them.

In some of these great towers are hollow statues of gold which seem giants and all manner of gold artefacts, even gold that seems like wooden logs to burn. Here dwell men who deal in markets of coffee and sugar and vast numbers of other like commodities. They have eyes in their shoulders, mouths in the middle of their breasts, a long train of hair grows backwards between their shoulders. They sit on finely-made leather cushions and there are also men like porters to carry food to them on magnificent plates of gold and silver.

In the uppermost rooms of these towers, which are as we would call palaces, sit stockbrokers, their bodies anointed with white powdered gold blown through hollow canes until they are shining all over. Above their heads hang the skulls of dead company directors, all hung and decked with feathers. Here they sit drinking, hundreds of them together, for as many as six or seven days at a time.

• • •

I am squatting on the verandah in the hot yellow afternoon making spills for my grandfather. I tear strips from the *Berbice Advertiser* as he's shown me and fold them carefully into tiny pleats. In the yard is the Po' Boy tree which is supposed to be lucky. Children late for school stop to touch it and recite:

> Pity pity Po' Boy
> Sorry fi me
> If God don' help me
> The devil surely will.

My grandfather rests in his chair, one foot up on the long wooden arm. I want to please him so I place four spills for his pipe on the wicker table at his side but he hardly notices. I try to peek at the hand that has two fingers missing but it is folded in his lap in such a way that I can't see properly.

Aunt Rosa comes out of the living-room to give me a glass of soursop:

'Tomorrow your daddy is coming to take you back to England.'

'England. England. England,' I dance along the verandah.

'Come in out of the sun, chile. You're gettin' all burnt up. I will take you over to the da Silvas to play one last time.'

I stop short, filled with apprehension, and start to scuff my shoe on the floor:

'I don' want to go.' I follow her inside where it is darker and cooler.

'What is this foolishness? Why you don' want to go?'

I don't want to tell her. I try to distract her attention from the da Silvas:

'What does my daddy do in London?'

'He works for Booker-McConnell, of course, in a big building called Plantation House in the City of London.' There is a note of pride in her voice which encourages me to lead her further away from the subject of the da Silvas:

'Will you show me the photograph of the men in London again?'

Aunt Rosa goes over to the large, carved oak dresser. She is darker than my father but with the same large creole eyes. Her black hair is in a roll at the front. On top of the dresser are some of my favourite objects: a tumbler full of glass swizzle sticks, a bell jar, glass goblets and, best of all, a garishly painted wooden Chinese god with a face like a gargoyle and a chipped nose. I hang around the edge fingering the carved roses while Aunt Rosa rummages in the drawer:

'Here it is. These men are very important. They are the men who meet every day to fix the price of sugar on the world market.'

She shows a photograph of dull, sombre-suited men with white faces gathered round a table and points to one of them:

'This is the man who owns the company your daddy works for.'

I try to look interested but I can feel the time running out. I am right.

'Now what is all this nonsense about the da Silvas?' she asks.

'I hate the da Silvas. They keep callin' me "ice-cream face".' And I burst into tears.

Later that night I lie in bed under a single sheet. The doors to the adjoining room are fixed back and I can hear Aunt Rosa talking to Mrs Hunter:

'Look how she fair-skinned, Frank's daughter. No one would ever know. An' she complainin' about it.' They laugh and lower their voices, but I can still hear fragments. Mrs Hunter is talking in a troubled voice about her brother:

'. . . the first coloured officer in the British Army . . . imagine how proud . . . other officers would not speak to him . . . the men refused to obey his orders . . . Some incident . . . trumped up, I tell you . . . an excuse . . . cashiered . . . the shock that ran through the family.' I hear the sob in her voice and Aunt Rosa hush-hushing her.

I creep out of bed towards the open doors. Moonlight floods over the leaves of the Molucca pear tree and spills through the jalousies onto the floor, a dark lake of polished wood. Stepping delicately over it is Salamander, the pale, golden gazelle of a cat, thin with pointy ears. He seems to be dancing some sort of minuet, extending each paw, then with a hop tapping the floor. Delighted, I move to take a closer look. And then I see it. Between his paws is a huge cockroach, a great black ugly thing lying on its back, its feelers moving this way and that. I must have squawked because there is a pause in the conversation, then Aunt Rosa says:

'Get back to bed, chile. If you look out of the window on a night like this you will see Moongazer at the cross-roads.'

'Hullo, ice-cream face.' It is my father and he is laughing as he lifts me way up into the sky and sing-chants:

> Molasses, molasses
> Sticky sticky goo
> Molasses, molasses
> Will always stick to you.

My aunts, uncles and cousins are standing round by the wooden lattice at the front of the house. Everyone is laughing and I laugh too.

●   ●   ●

Some time afterwards, in England, I am playing with my doll Lucy in a garden full of browns and greys. Lucy's face is cracked like crazy paving because I left her out in the rain but I love her because her hair is the colour of golden syrup. The cockney boy who lives next door has climbed into the pear tree on his side of the fence and is intoning in a sneery voice:

'Your fahver looks like a monkey.

Your fahver looks like a monkey.'

I go inside and tell my mother:

'Mum, Keith says Daddy looks like a monkey. And I think so too.'

My mother stops beating the cake mixture. She looks sad but not the way she looks when she is sad herself. It is the way she looks when she is teaching me what to be sad about:

'Ahh,' she says, as if I have grazed my knee. 'Well don't tell Daddy, you know he would be so hurt.'

·　　　　　·　　　　　·

They are lost, Wat, his father and the ragged remnants of the crew. They are padding the small craft which the Arawaks have named 'the eight-legged sea-spider', and they are lost in a labyrinth of rivers, a confluence of streams that branch into rapids and then into more billowing waters all crossing the other, ebbing and flowing. They seem to travel far on the same spot so that it takes an hour to travel a stone's cast. The sun appears in the sky in three places at once and whether they attempt to use the sun as a guide or a compass they are carried in circles amongst a multitude of islands.

·　　　　　·　　　　　·

I am fourteen and back from England for the summer. My friend Gail Fraser has pestered and pestered her mother to cook labba for me before I return.

Now we sit at the dinner table, Gail's great-aunt Bertha, her mother, her brother Edmund, and me and Gail. Great-aunt Bertha is a yellowy-skinned woman whose face is all caught up in leathery pouches under her white wavy hair. Gail's mother is square-jawed with iron-grey crinkly hair and she is too practical for my liking as I judge everybody by how much 'soul' they have. My friend Gail is honey-coloured and round as a butterball. She has brown almond eyes and curly brown hair and scores about eight out of ten for soul. We have spent most of the holiday lying on her bed exchanging passionate secrets and raiding the rumbly old fridge for plum-juice. My deepest secret is that I am so in love with her brother Edmund that I could die. Edmund has what I call a crème de cacao complexion, tight black curls, full lips with the first black hairs of a moustache. He is slim and has black eyes that are brimful of soul. I know he would respond to me if he would stop talking about cricket for ONE minute. As it is, I have to be content to breathe the same air as him, which is pretty nice in itself.

Gail and I are trying desperately not to scream out loud with laughter as great-aunt Bertha chides Edmund for not wearing his jacket:

'My father would not see the boys at dinner without their jackets.'

Dreadful snorts are coming out of Gail and Edmund is pulling faces. I can't look up. Gail is heaving and shaking next to me. Great-aunt Bertha turns to me:

'When I was in London I used to look after a sick. She was a real lady. I was her companion. I would have liked to stay in England. I asked to stay but they wouldn't let me.'

Gail explodes and runs out of the room. Her mother looks disapproving. I manage to hang on to myself.

That evening Edmund takes Gail and me in the rowing-boat to the middle of Canje Creek because Gail insists that I drink creek water and I won't drink from the edge because it's too muddy and slimy. We row out onto the midnight black and glittering waters of the creek. It is silent apart from a goat-sucker bird calling 'hoo yoo, hoo yoo' in the distance.

'This time tomorrow I'll be in London.'

'What will you be doing?' asks Gail.

'I don't know. I might be in a coffee bar with my friends playing the juke-box.'

'Play something for me.'

'What?'

' "Blue-suede Shoes" by Elvis Presley.'

'Oh phooey that's old. They won't still have it.' I can tell that she is hurt. I am sitting behind Edmund. I kiss him on the back of his shoulder so lightly he doesn't notice. Gail grasses me up:

'She kissin' you, Edmund.' He ignores me.

I lean over the edge of the boat, cup my hands and scoop up some of the water. It is clear and refreshing.

'Now you must come back,' says Gail. 'Now you're bound to come back.' And her voice is full of spite.

●   ●   ●

Wearied and scorched, they bury Wat as best they can in the muddy bank of the creek. His father's demeanour is grim and he says no prayers. They just sit around for a bit. After they have gone, dead leaves, twigs, bark and moss begin to float and fall onto the burial spot, the first signs of rain. Seed-pods plummet and burst on the water and heavy raindrops start to pock the surface of the creek. Out on the lake torrential rains flatten the reeds at the water's edge. Everything turns grey. Wat's body, loosened from its grave, begins a quest of its own through the network of creeks and streams and rivers.

A month later, Wat's father gives up his search for the tantalising city of El Dorado and writes in his log:

'It's time to leave Guiana to the sun whom they worship and steer northwards.'

•   •   •

I am back at last. The old metal bucket of a ferry dips in the sweet brown waters of the Berbice River, passes Crab Island and ties up at the stelling.

I walk through the town to the house. The Po' Boy tree is still there but the house looks ramshackle, sagging on its rigid wooden stilts, the wood where the paint has peeled, grey from the sun.

I haven't told my aunts I'm coming. I'm going to surprise them. I go up the steps to the front door and announce myself through the open slats of the jalousies. There is no sign of life.

'It's me. Frank's daughter,' I say, in case in their old age they have forgotten my name.

Through the slatted door I see a shape. It is one of my aunts. She doesn't open the door. I peer through. She is swaying and wringing her hands.

'Avril. It's me. Open the door.'

I can hear her moaning softly:

'Oh this is disastrous. Oh this is disastrous. Deep trouble. We in deep trouble.'

Finally she opens the door. I hear Aunt Rosa's voice on the telephone, shriller than I remembered it:

'I tell you it's a plot, Laura. They're lying to you. They're all on drugs. Don' believe them.' She hangs up and turns around. Both of them are neatly dressed in blouses and slacks. Aunt Rosa's hair is still in the same black roll at the front but her face has shrunk with age and her eyes are blazing:

'So you've come back. I suppose you want our money. Well you're unlucky. We haven't got any.'

We go into the living-room. The place is in dusty disorder. Aunt Rosa stands by the window, angry and troubled:

'I didn't want you to see us like this. Why did you come? We all busted up over here. The family is all busted up. Laura is in the hospital with some kinda sclerosis. She's twisted up in the bed like a hermit crab and all the doctors and nurses are on drugs, I can see it in their eyes.'

Avril is moving about, muttering, picking up things and putting them down again, pulling at the frizzy hair round her dark impassive face:

'STOP STILL FOR ONE MINUTE WILL YOU, AVRIL?' screams Aunt Rosa. 'Your niece is here from England. Don't you remember her? We raised her and then she left.'

'Where's Auntie Florence?' I ask timidly.

'We had to send her up to Canada to your uncle Bertie's. She livin' in the past. She talkin' to the dead. She thinks they're still alive. She anxious and upset all the time. She thought everything in the house was on fire. Even us, her sisters. She saw us burnin' up burnin' up like paper, black with a red edge. Paper sisters. She's turned into a screwball.'

She moves over to the sofa and sits there gripping her walking-stick and turning it round and round. I try to think of somebody who could help:

'What about the Frasers? Do you still see them?'

'Oh they left a long time ago, Toronto, New Orleans, somewhere. They all left. I didn't think my brothers would leave but they did. They all left and married white, street-walkin' bitches. They left us behind because we were too dark.'

She leans forward and speaks passionately:

'I loved my brothers. My brothers are innocent. It's their wives that keep them from us. Especially that red-headed bitch that stole Bertie. Mind you, Bertie could charm a cobra. Bertie could charm a camoodie. She drugs Bertie, you know, so that he can't come back.'

She sniffs the air:

'I can smell somethin',' she says suddenly.

'What?'

'Somethin' I shouldn't be smellin',' she snaps. She is glaring at me suspiciously:

'You don' look like you used to.'

'How not?'

'You used to have brown eyes.'

'No I didn't. Look, there's a photo of me on the dresser. I always had blue eyes.' I go and get it. It's dusty like everything else. The sight of it throws her into a venomous rage:

'Just because you've got white skin and blue eyes you think you haven't got coloured blood in you. But you have. Just like me. It's in your veins. You can't escape from it. There's mental illness in the family too.'

I am shocked. She continues in an unstoppable outburst:

'You sent your father's ashes back here because he had mixed blood. You were too ashamed to let him stay in England. And you're blackmailing your cousin over there for the same reason. If anyone finds out he'll lose his job! Why do you do these terrible things? You were a nice chile. Why do you do all these terrible things?'

'Do you have anything to drink in the fridge?' My stomach is churning.

'I don' know. Go and look. Everything's gone middly-muddly over here.'

I open the fridge door and recoil. Inside, the contents are webbed with mould from all the electricity cuts. I go back to the living-room:

'Tomorrow I'll fix for somebody to come in and help you.'

'We don' want strangers pokin' their noses in, seeing what's happened to us.' She lowers her head then jerks it up:

'Your father's skin was whiter than mine. If he'd been my colour your mother never would have married him!'

'Rosa. We're in the nineteen-eighties. Nobody cares about that sort of thing any more.'

'You think I'm crazy?' she sneers. I go over to Avril to give her a hug. She pushes me away:

'I'm not the affectionate type,' she says. 'Oh, this is terrible. This is really awful.'

'AVRIL YOU'RE A DONKEY,' shouts Aunt Rosa. 'She's mentally ill too. She's ashamed of her illness. She hasn't left the house for a year. She too frighten'. I do the shopping.

Everything was fine until January the fifth, then it all stopped.'
Avril starts to mumble a litany of potential disasters:

'What will happen when she leaves? There will be all those
people in the street. What will she do? And it might rain. She
might get wet.'

'I hope she melts,' snarls Aunt Rosa.

Suddenly, she puts her head in her hands:

'I don' know what's happened to us,' she says.

That night I try and sleep. The room is musty. The sheet is damp
with humidity. The mosquito net has holes all over. Through
the night I hear one or other of them pacing the house. I
half-sleep and doze because it gets into my head that they might
set fire to my room.

It is evening when I reach Georgetown. The great house is just as
I remember it.

The sight of Evelyn at the door fills me with relief. I notice the
fine net of grey over her coarse tight curls.

'Goodness, Evelyn. My aunts have gone crazy in New
Amsterdam.'

'So I hear. Well you know what they say. All the mad people
are in Berbice. You should come back here for good. Not just for
your aunts. There is so much to do here to turn this country
round.'

I follow her up the old circular wooden staircase. Sitting on
the steps half-way up is a black woman in a loose skirt. Next to
her are two sacks marked: 'US Famine Aid. Destination
Ethiopia.' Evelyn sees my curious stare:

'You are shocked? She's a smuggler from the Corentyne. We
past shame in this country. There are people for whom crime is
still a shock. We way past that stage. Way past. That is wheat
flour she tryin' to sell.'

We go into the large kitchen and Evelyn fetches me a glass of
freshly-squeezed grapefruit juice. It tastes deliciously bitter and
cool after the hot journey.

'Have you got a match, Evelyn?' I'm waving a cigarette in the
air.

'You din' bring matches?' She laughs. 'You have forgotten
what it is like to live in a country that is bankrupt. There is no

milk in the country. Dried milk costs twelve US dollars a bag. Money has left the banks. Money is dancin' around in the streets. The black market rules here now. Come and I will show you which room you are staying in. The others are in a political meeting downstairs. They said they will see you in the morning.'

In my room I fix the mosquito net. Evelyn is leaning against the door jamb:

'You have everything you need?'

'Yes. Thanks. I'm going to bed, now. I'm exhausted. We'll talk in the morning.'

'You know,' says Evelyn, 'you should stay. If the party could get hold of two hundred thousand US dollars we could turn this country round. I will get it somehow. I am telling you, this place could be a paradise.'

After she has gone I peer through the jalousies. Outside is a sugar-apple tree and dragon-tongue shrubs by the brick path below. In the yard I can see the rusted shells of two cars.